# the still life

I0638681

a novel by
D. Mark Gabel

©1997-2006, D. Mark Gabel
all rights reserved

ISBN 978-0-6151-3479-6

Originally written on an Apple® Macintosh® PowerPC 6100/60av using Adobe® PageMaker® 5.0 and continued sporadically through an evolution of Apples, lap and desk, through final fruition on the 2006 Intel® iMac® with Adobe InDesign® CS2. The typefaces are Adobe ITC Garamond and Apple's elegant Zapfino.

D. MARK GABEL

CentaurDesign.net

DMGabel@CentaurDesign.net
919.308.2709

The balance of our lives depends greatly on the people around us. My life is filled with those who believe in me, and I gratefully acknowledge the difference they have made in my efforts and my perspective.

Thank you George D. & Juanita B. Gabel, my parents, for naming me to be an author and guiding me in the ways of education, art, and possibilities.

Thank you Elysia, Malaine, & Marcus, my children, for assuming that your Daddy's projects were all amazing and for coming to me with your questions, large and small.

Thank you Adriana van Stralen, my wife, for coming into my life and for your continual love, support, and trust.

Thank you Dan & Jackie DeProspero, sensei & sempai, for continuing my study of kyudo and its deeper meanings.

Finally, thank you Charleen Swansea, for your confidence, faith, and elegant Southern sense of humor.

—David Mark Gabel
Hillsborough, North Carolina, 2006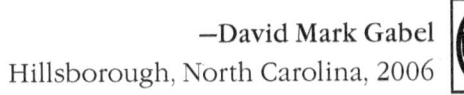

*"Music and poetry sprang from our weapon. The bow is the old first lyre, the monochord, the initial rune of fine art, and is as inseparably connected with the history of culture as are the alphabets of the learned languages. The humanities grew out from archery as a flower from a seed.*

*"No sooner did the soft, sweet note of the bow-string charm the ear of genius than music was born, and from music came poetry and painting and sculpture."*

—Maurice Thompson,
*The Witchery of Archery,* 1879

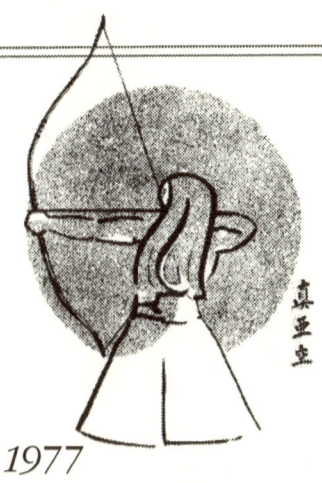

1977

# Kyoto

*Patience. Strength without tension.*

*I slowly drew the Japanese bow, an elegant bamboo-sheathed nisun yumi, in the spreading apart of the hands to the full draw of modern kyudo. At full draw, or kai (meeting), my energy was fully rooted deep in the earth even as it expanded upward to the heavens and horizontally through the arrow and my body, creating the tautness that concentrates resources, connecting the inner to the outer. Ki, or energy, built from within my core until the arrow released itself (hanare), my gloved right hand loosing the string naturally and explosively, the yumi quickly rotating in my hand until the string touched the back of my arm, the bamboo arrow (ya) punching into the core of the 36 centimeter kasumi (mist) target twenty-eight meters distant. Then zanshin (remaining spirit) sent energy to the target while expanding in all other directions, calmly balancing my spirit like the reverberations in a bell after it has been struck. I lowered the bow, drew my feet from their wide stance back to the center, stepped away from the shooting line, bowing to the kaimidana before stepping outside the shooting area of the dojo.*

*"Ma" is the pronunciation of the Japanese character that means "interval." Ma is the white space in a black-ink painting, a white space defined by the guided darkness of the painter's skill. It is also felt when the brush, correctly ink-laden, is placed to the paper, determining the power and flow of the stroke. Power is shown by our willingness to use the strength*

*of the black to define the purity of the white, clear in our intentions and responsibility.*

*Ma is also the rest in a piece of music, the purposefulness of proper movements in a tea ceremony, the juxtaposing of blossoms in a flower arrangement.*

*Any meditative art, or indeed any task, makes use of ma, both in the performance of an action and in the beauty of the finished work, merging us with our actions and our respected tools.*

*Ma determines when the arrow is loosed.*

Kelly green moss overflowing the rough stone edge of the small sculpted fountain's bowl, the lush growth saturated with fine mist in this remote part of the garden. Dappled light through the bamboo leaves reflecting from small and continuous splashes, diamonds of light. The white of the stone, the clarity of the flowing water, the deep green of the moss juxtaposed against the lighter pliable green of the overhanging delicate leaves, the shadowed background of the stalks.

*Click.*

Another exposed negative, perhaps a starting point for a large display print, settled in composition, evocative in the play of light and shadow, with hours in the darkroom to follow. Perhaps a painting. Perhaps both.

I am an artist. It took a long time to admit that, both to myself and others, because it seemed a rather grandiose statement to make, like I was comparing myself to those whose work I held in awe. Once my art began to sell, though, it seemed unfair to those who actually paid for my work to deny the label and I gradually became comfortable with the idea. Inside, though, the label didn't matter—I just did what I had to do.

My mother sent me to study with different artists from the age of eleven. I studied pastels, ink, charcoal, acrylics, pencil, oils and photography, in varied places across the United States, and then studied sumi-e type watercolors with a Chinese gentleman—all this before, during, and after college, one form leading to another to allow another unique form of expression, feeling, intensity, tone. I had other interests as well, but it seemed as though I always practiced some form of fine art. For example, my watercolor studies led me to photography when my teacher showed me his camera and explained that I needed to keep a record of my paintings before I sold them—it wasn't long before photography became another medium, independent of visual record-keeping.

Every art form has its limitations, and every artist must remain aware. A painter who daubs oil paint will look for subjects that best exploit the richness and depth of the thick color on canvas, while a potter must always keep the clay at its proper thickness to avoid disaster in the kiln, limiting the choices of form. Each form also has commonalities, techniques requiring control of the medium merged with the intuition and freedom to spontaneously express. The techniques of each art form are unique and alike at the same time, and it's important to be able to recognize which subjects are appropriate to which medium. Techniques were information for me, and I was careful to remain aware that information is not knowledge, for knowledge implies an assimilation into my innermost depths. Wisdom? I can be patient for wisdom.

It's my job to see, then communicate that seeing, that vision—it's all part of the same process. Translating what speaks to me into a form that then perhaps speaks to others. Trusting that vision is important, for it keeps me in touch with my art, keeps my work fresh. How fortunate for me that my work seems to resonate with others.

Though only twenty-six I had built enough of a market to let an agent handle sales while I studied ink painting, or sumi-e, in Japan. I came to Kyoto four years ago on a special visa, and when I won an honorable mention in the annual sumi-e art show after less than nine months, my sensei got me into the professional painters' association, opening new doors.

Kimiko arranged her cup and saucer exactly in the center of her place setting, easily, with studied care. "So how is it that you study kyudo as well, Maaku-san?" Maaku was as close to pronouncing Marcus as she could come—true with most people here—but I was accustomed to the odd pronunciation now.

My Japanese was fair but Kimiko's English was far better—one of the reasons I liked her as an acquaintance and as a language teacher.

It was cool and dimly lit inside the New Bluegrass coffee house, the music muted for the sparse mid-afternoon crowd. Japanese coffeehouses have always been refuges well-suited to conversation and study, at least until the devoted music lovers converge in the evenings. Sometimes it was good for us to have our class here.

Answering, I said, "I've always studied archery in one form or another, starting with Boy Scouts, so I immediately researched what was available when I arrived in Japan. Discovering yabusame excited me. The thought of shooting a bow while riding a horse reminded me of history's great horse-archer cultures, a way to cooperate with another being instead of competing. Until I came to Japan I had no idea mounted archery was still taught anywhere in the world." As a Japanese, she understood the unique nature of yabusame, a rare art created for the Imperial court and only demonstrated in public twice a year.

"You see, when I came to Japan I knew I wanted to study archery as a martial art, but since I've always been close to animals, the concept of a martial art that included a special connection with an animal excited me. Since yabusame takes many years and the proper connections to study, I began practicing traditional standing archery from a modern teacher with Ogasawara training. I also started riding horses one day a week to prepare." Ogasawara is one of only two types of mounted archery still practiced.

"I still ride horses and love to be out in the countryside," I continued, "but I haven't pursued a study of yabusame, studying the more modern and slightly less ceremonial form of kyudo instead. Over the years, in fact, kyudo has become more than enough to keep me occupied. I did go to a couple of yabusame ceremonies and was enjoyed them, but my kyudo sensei has become important to me, and I wouldn't want to leave him, no matter how special the alternative." I had risen to sandan, or third degree, since beginning the study of kyudo.

She stroked her cup idly with a fingertip, and said, "The differences between your country and mine are so great. I have heard that in America, a true teacher-student relationship is often misunderstood, that there is often an aloof and impersonal separation between the two."

I nodded. "Many Americans students can't understand how the two flow together, how dependent learning is upon teaching. They don't see the essence of *ma*." Kimiko and I both knew that Shinto was more pervasive than Zen in this culture, was in fact Japan's original and indigenous religion, a belief system that stretched far back over the centuries. We also knew the two complemented each other as few philosophies ever could. Part of the Japanese way of life was the importance of the teacher-student relationship, a willingness for the student to subjugate personal desires to the tutelage of the sensei.

"It's difficult to explain, but after I studied kyudo for a while, I began to notice a new timing to my brush strokes. If I was absolutely ready, the brush would make exactly the right movement on the paper, and the ink would flow easily, exactly as I envisioned it doing before I began. I began to feel my art, and I enjoyed the entire process, from the purity of blank white paper to delivery of the finished painting. Art and archery began to feed off one another, and one day I realized something inside me was guiding the arrow, that I was connected to it all the way to the target. I believe I fully understand now why warriors were always required to study painting, or flower arrangement, or the tea ceremony."

"And your study now?..."

"I paint watercolors, photograph and practice sumi-e every day, of course, and send paintings home to an agent for sale, but I also practice kyudo most every evening, and I visit with an old arrowmaker friend a few times a week." I finished my coffee. "Would you like another cup?"

"Yes, please." I signaled the waiter.

Kimiko was silent, looking down into her coffee. "You know it's very unusual for a young artist to sell work in Japan. Usually it's only allowed after years and years of study."

"I know, Kimiko-san," I said. "It's only because I am gaijin, an outsider, and because my sumi sensei knew that I was already established before I began study with him. I suppose I'm an outsider in many ways..."

After I left Kimiko I took the streetcar, getting off at the stop on the shopping street near home. I decided to take a break and play the arcade Tank game on the sidewalk, as I often did when it was convenient. The game was under the awning in front of a small restaurant where I was well-known, and, as usual, I was joined by young boys watching me play, deeply interested.

I was fascinated by the green vector graphics on the black background, and I was amazed that computer chips could generate a feeling of driving a tank inside a physical maze while I engaged in a battle with my electronic opponent. It was light years ahead of the Pong game that was the rage when I'd left the States. Even now, nevertheless, I knew there was a future for computers beyond these games, knew their time was going to come. Perhaps, I thought, one day computers wouldn't be limited to the punch cards now used in businesses and colleges; maybe somehow they'd be made easier to use.

*I slowly rotated the hardened bamboo shaft in my hands, marveling at its smoothness and balance. The damascened steel blade mounted on the front was a narrow broadhead, rather unusual for a traditional Japanese design. The three feathers used to fletch the shaft were ivory-white for two-thirds of their five-inch length, merging into a brown that matched the color of the shaft. The feathers were tied to the arrow with ivory-colored silk wrapped seamlessly in short lengths around the leading and trailing edges of the feathers. The nock set into the back end of the shaft was made of horn, again in a matching brown, again wrapped with clear-lacquered silk where it mated to the bamboo. The utter simplicity and beauty of this arrow spoke to me deep in my soul. To study this arrow was a joy, but I was also left with the feeling of artistic inadequacy, the knowledge that I would never be able to make anything so full of grace, so unified.*

*I laid it down next to its mate and next to the three other matched pairs in the red-lacquered box. Hiroshu sensei, the arrowmaker, smiled.*

*I inspected the other arrows, which were all made of highly burnished hardwoods without fletching. Each of the other shafts had matching objects attached to either end without a nock at the rear—something I had never seen. One pair had blades, the next had two-inch-long steel tips rounded at the ends, and the final pair trailed a small cylindrical steel bar on a three-inch silk cord from each end. Again, the workmanship was flawless, the color of the shafts matching over the entire set, small kanji on each marking the maker. The steel had a mirrorlike finish, and everything fit together as if its unity were a preordained thing. After I had reverently replaced the final shaft, I bowed low to the maker.*

"What amazing arrows these are, sensei, but I am not familiar with these types of points. And these three pairs have no nocking ends. I've never seen anything like this."

"Indeed. Indeed. Please, come with me. I feel like walking through the shrine grounds. Tie your hair back, as if for kyudo. You may come barefoot, but leave your camera here."

Hiroshu sensei lived in the back of a small temple adjacent to the grounds of the ancient Japanese capital at Nara, a short train ride from Kyoto, and he loved to walk through its grounds and gardens. Most tourists came to the main grounds, famous for small deer trained to bow for a cracker, but his area was not for the public. The traditional grounds with their petting-zoo atmosphere might as well have been worlds away from us.

It was early summer, the cherry blossom festivals only a month past. Seemingly placed at random intervals, the trees billowed out into a gentle canopy above. The wind blew the now fully green leaves just enough to make an ever-changing pattern of shadows in the bright sun, while gently swaying the chimes that hung at the corners of the veranda surrounding the temple. The whispering of the breeze mingled with the music of the chimes—and also, if I listened closely, with the constant splattering sound of water as it flowed against the large smooth stones at the bottom of a small nearby waterfall.

The raked gravel pathway wound its way through moss-covered rocks and up to occasional tiny, arched wooden bridges crossing narrow streams that seemed to merge and separate with studied abandon.

Hiroshu sensei, my teacher and mentor, knew how much I loved to walk barefoot and he indulged me whenever he could. Going without shoes is not unheard of in the martial arts, but it requires a foot-washing ritual when returning indoors.

I was dressed in jeans and a lightweight long-sleeved shirt, sleeves rolled to just below the elbows. The stones on the path were rounded and small, and I chose each step with care, in a way a friend had shown me when we were together in college. I was amazed how much more spiritual each step felt when I was shoeless, setting each foot down gently and quietly. I felt so grounded. When she showed me how to walk this way, it was specifically to teach me how to walk quietly through the underbrush as the Native Americans had, but this flat-footed style of walking appealed to me from the first step. Not only was it quiet, but I could feel each step, really feel it.

I knew Hiroshu sensei wouldn't tell me about the arrows until he was ready, that he wouldn't have shown them to me unless he wanted to tell me about them. If I had asked him, he would just have shushed me again, so I concentrated on our walk.

"How are things at home, Maaku-san?"

"Fine, sensei. I hired a housekeeper a few weeks ago, and everything is going very well. She has quickly exceeded my expectations and become very valuable to me. Most of the time I don't even know she's there, but she takes care of everything.

"She keeps an eye on my supplies and replaces them for me before I even know I need them. She also keeps my records and is learning my gaijin preferences in food. She's even gotten over the fact that I fast every Thursday."

I was about five-foot nine, weighed one-hundred seventy-five pounds, and had been a vegetarian for ten years. Food and drink were not my consuming passions.

"Good, good. Is your business doing well?"

"Oh, yes, very well, thank you." Only a sensei would ask such personal questions, but I knew it was a mark of his concern for me.

"Do you have much free time these days?"

"I can have as much free time as needed, sensei. Is there anything I can do for you?"

I was concerned now, because the concept of free time was central to Japanese culture. Relationships were a delicate thing, and offending someone was easy if you weren't very careful. The only way to gracefully bow out of an offer that someone made was to plead a lack of free time, and for someone to ask if you had free time before making an offer was most unusual. Now, whatever he was about to suggest, I wouldn't be able to turn down. I was pre-committed. I owed him a great deal, however, and knew I would do anything he asked.

"For me, no. But for yourself, perhaps. Walk with me now, and we will talk of private things."

Japanese culture is filled with secrets in every ancient field of study, so I wasn't surprised at what he said, though his tone seemed more serious than usual. Sensei had, in fact, already shown me some secrets of his arrowmaker's art.

Almost everything I learned in sumi-e or kyudo—whether it involved either information or perception—was a secret at some level, but this was more serious—I sensed something larger here. I also felt some trepidation, for this concerned the martial arts, and was formal. Any information offered carried a responsibility, and I knew that the greater the secret, the greater the duty. Finally, though, I was not concerned, for I knew that after all else was said and done, I trusted him.

We continued on our walk, gradually circling through the grounds. He spoke of the different schools of kyudo and their origins—from the strength-oriented bushido styles to the more elegant and ceremonial Ogasawara style, and the variations of each; he spoke of how the arrows differed according to their purposes.

I already knew a little of what he told me, but many things were new.

There was information about flaming arrows, some used for offense and others that were not offensive, that were primarily for signaling at night, though all uses were in a military context. Fire on the end of a stick traveling through the air is an ominous thing in a country of wood and paper houses, and only the best archers were trusted with the responsibility of the fire arrows.

I had a glimpse of the strategy for signal-arrows, tools that could not fall into the hands of the enemy, that, like fire arrows, had to be protected at any cost. Whistling arrows were used primarily for signaling—different tones for different signals—and sensei presented a vivid mental picture of the tactics of ancient warfare for me.

As different military styles of shooting and strategy developed, each was linked to a distinct and separate formula for battle, even down to the way arrows were tied into the box-style back quivers—a fraction of a second advantage in nocking an arrow could be vital in battle.

Archery, I knew, had ceased to be a military resource with the advent of guns late in the sixteenth century, but to the credit of this culture the art had been kept intact as a spiritual training art in an unbroken historical line. Though earlier attempts had been made, it wasn't until after World War II that a nationwide organization was formed, merging the traditional schools of ceremony and of war into the modern form of kyudo, which was now the main form of study.

Hiroshu sensei continued with stories of how single archers had changed the outcome of battles, and how a just one well-placed shaft had changed the political, religious, or even artistic history and direction of a region, or even the entire country. Many of these stories were known by serious students of the art, and he told them well. The ones I hadn't heard fascinated me, while the ones I heard before were cast in a new light.

He was building an image of the individual archer that evoked a sense of pride in our art, a substantial picture of the importance and honor each warrior must feel as he risks his life on internal or external command. Archers—always in the thick of battle, always exposing themselves to the possibility of death.

"You know, Maaku-san, don't you, that every move in a martial art has a countermove, and every form of attack has a defense?"

"Yes, sensei."

"Have you never wondered, then, about the defenses against your arrows?"

"Well, sensei, I know that most armor is useless against a properly placed arrow. Didn't mounted warriors once wear silk cloaks that would billow out behind them, because an arrow's energy would not penetrate the waving cloak as it would a more solid target? And don't some forms of other martial arts, such as aikido or karatedo, teach how to deflect arrows?"

"Yes, of course. But how else do you think an archer would protect himself?"

"Traditionally, didn't archers also carry swords?"

"Traditionally, yes." He was silent for a few moments.

"With your interest in becoming an archer, then, do you think it would be in your best interest to study swords and swordplay?"

"Of course, sensei. I would be honored to study kendo or iaido, or anything else you or Henmi sensei think proper."

"Your kyudo sensei and I have been discussing this, and we think it is time. You will not be expected to become as expert with the swords as you are with the bow, but it is a skill that must become familiar to you. It should be part of your training."

I felt immense gratitude for the responsibility, tempted for a moment to put that feeling into extravagant words. I knew, however, that such a gesture would be unnecessary and even excessive. He was offering me something special, true, but also charging me with an extreme amount of duty. If I added these new studies and failed, it would dishonor both of us.

"As important as swordplay has been to our culture, you can imagine that many styles of study have been developed over the centuries, and perhaps you wouldn't be surprised to learn there is a style specifically related to swords and kyudo. Shortly, we will introduce you to a sensei who specializes in teaching the art of the sword specifically for archers. You will study with him three times a week—enough to learn the basics, but a light enough schedule to leave you time for kyudo and sumi-e."

"Thank you, Hiroshu sensei," I said, keeping any expectations or doubts to myself, as expected.

As we returned to sensei's house, he directed me around to the veranda overlooking his garden, so I would not yet have to wash my feet. I sat on the edge of the polished wood, my feet resting on the smooth garden rocks, my back resting against a warm wooden post. His garden was a very serene place, one of my favorites, and I closed my eyes to feel the sun's warmth while I waited for him. He would serve the light green tea himself, I knew.

This garden wasn't very large, of course—most aren't. It was only about the size of a large living room, but was surrounded by hedges inside solid wooden fencing and was very private.

Sensei came out on to the veranda and placed the tray between us. We drank our ocha in silence.

"So, Maaku-san, we have covered the physical aspects of an archer as warrior, have we not?"

"Yes, sensei."

"So. Now I will ask you again: Have you never wondered about the defenses an archer must have? Please think before answering."

By the way he phrased the question, he meant I already knew the answer, and that it did not deal with the physical aspects of archery, which had never dealt with anything defensive. So I thought for a few minutes, concentrating on the process of shooting. I thought particularly of how I to direct my ki to move with the arrow when released.

"Are we speaking of things relating to ki?"

"Of course."

I closed my eyes, crossed my legs in a half-lotus, and imagined I was shooting my bow, but with a person as the target instead of a piece of paper. It was the first time I had ever done so.

I thought of that person-target as an aware being, adept at martial arts. I then imagined myself as the target, facing the archer. I felt the energy, or ki, that was basic to my studies, felt it grow, flow, and release towards me, another new thought.

"Do you mean that if I can direct my ki to move with the arrow, someone else could feel it as well?"

Sensei clapped. "Yes!"

He began to explain. "In ways, it is easier to defend yourself against one who understands and uses ki than against one who does not. As in all martial arts, if a person sends something out, then another person can pick it up. When the aggressor's focus is as tight as it should be, then all the aware target must do is move out of the way—and be where the arrow is not. This will also be a part of your sword training, because it is a basic concept. Up until now you have only been concerned with the offensive nature of things, so to speak."

I thought about it, then said "What if the archer is a master?"

"Oh, that would be very different, unless the target were also a master, for a master is connected to everything all the time, and his intentions cannot be felt, unless he wishes. But that is not something for you to consider yet, Maaku-san. Let us speak instead of things on a more basic level, if we may."

I nodded almost imperceptibly.

"Tell me what you have learned about ki on a day-to-day level, please."

"I use it every day in my painting, of course. I couldn't imagine practicing sumi-e without ki directing each brush stroke. When I paint or practice sumi-e or kyudo, I work to hold mushin, no-mindedness, so things may direct themselves. That has become an important part of my life.

"I've been noticing some unusual developments over the past months, sensei. I'm not sure if they relate to ki, but I haven't been able to talk with anyone who may understand. I realize these aren't basic issues, sensei, but it would help if I could talk to someone I trusted."

"Go on," he said.

I took a breath. "Maybe I'm making too much of it, but often I seem to be able to see a person's intentions. By that I mean if someone is walking down the street, I know whether he is going to turn or go straight. It's not usually obvious, but I've noticed that if he turns on impulse—into a store, for example—instead of following his original intentions, I see an almost imperceptible image of him continuing on his original path. Does this make sense?"

"Yes, it does." Sensei was silent for a few moments. "What else?"

"Well, sensei," I continued. "I suppose it started with my painting, but it seems I've developed the ability to sort of see the entire painting before I start."

"Is that so unusual, Maaku-san?"

"Not by itself, sensei, but this seems different. Let me give you an example.

"I've never studied sculpture, but it's something I've considered from time to time, even though I know this might not be the right time in my life. Still, I'm drawn to textures and form, so thought it was a natural medium to draw my attention.

"I had the thought again recently, so actually sat down to try to imagine the process, much like I would if I were starting a new painting. Sensei, what I imagined just seemed so real—and not just the carving, either, but the feel of the tools, the space I worked in, every smallest detail.

"It was amazing, sensei. It was as if I had stepped out of my normal schedule and was participating in the whole undertaking outside of myself—I was actually living it. I was working in wood for this piece, and could see the grain, smell the odors release as the chisel peeled a curl away, actually feel the consistency and weight. I knew the decisions that would need to be made as they came up, I made choices, I learned as if I were actually carving a real sculpture.

"When I was done I not only knew the piece and could see it fully formed, but it was a part of my life. It couldn't have been more real if it had actually happened."

Hiroshu sensei considered for a few minutes. "Maaku-san, one of the responsibilities of any sensei is to judge a student's current state of understanding of the art being taught. If a new technique or understanding is given at the wrong time, the result could very well be catastrophic and actually set the student back.

"One of the greatest strengths of our way of teaching is to keep an eye out for the development of the entire person, not only as it relates to the art, but character and attitude as well.

"I now recognize that we should have spoken of these things before, and I apologize. I should have seen the signs that your understanding of life has changed."

Again he was quiet, obviously reflecting deeply on what he was about to say. Finally he began. "As a student's training progresses, certain thresholds are crossed. Some students only learn the basics and then go on with their lives—kyudo as it is taught to high school and university students will usually fall in this category. Other students learn more, so their discipline becomes a part of their lives, and they cannot go back to a state of not-knowing. The goal of a serious student, as you know, is to further his or her training to the personal limit, and once you reach a certain level then it has a bearing on every part of your life.

"You have connected yourself to others and their ki. That much is obvious. And you have done it without specific, formal training. The study of swords will further your training. I now feel we should have started it sooner. In this regard, there is something else you must now study as well, and this is the thing that will be private, the thing that will take your time."

"I'm sorry, sensei, but I thought you meant my sword training when you spoke of that which is private."

"Oh, no, to study sword would be natural and common, although somewhat unusual for gaijin, especially in conjunction with kyudo. No, what I mean is that now you must begin another form of study entirely, an art that is very secret. Once I present the idea of this training, you must either accept or reject it. If you accept it, it will go on to become an integral part of your daily life, a very important part. If you decide to reject it, nothing more will be said, and it will not be offered again."

"I understand, sensei, and I am honored you would consider me for this study."

"Good." He carried the tray into the house and back came out with the red-lacquered arrow box. He placed it between us, opening it so the sun shone off the gleaming metal at the ends of the eight arrows it contained. The details, the exquisite construction of these works of art were even more astounding in full sunlight. I had never seen anything that affected me so deeply.

"Maaku-san, these are some of the tools of yado, the Way of the Arrow."

*Secrets. My life became one secret after another after I accepted sensei's offer of study.*

*In practice I learned to whirl the yado arrows quickly and intricately, striking the practice dummy on a marked spot, the shafts whipping in a blur with each move.*

*The emphasis with the lightweight shafts was not to perform maneuvers that used brute strength, but rather to expertly hit exposed pressure points, tendons, and, in the case of the bladed shafts, blood vessels near the skin's surface. The basic moves, or kata, involved a technique known as tsurukai, or "cutting the bowstring." These moves are usually meant to disable an opponent, rendering him immediately helpless, as unable to function as a bow would be if its string were cut. Arrows could be thrown as well as shot or twirled, so there were also kata involving short-range throwing.*

*I practiced month after month, using combinations of one shaft or two, with a bow in hand and without, with a shooting glove and without, with standard kyudo arrows, with the Jo (staff), sword, or even a walking cane. Many of the techniques had their origins in iaido, the art of drawing the sword, and as such were begun and ended in less than the blink of an eye.*

*I was taught that yado had begun as it was presented to me, as a defense for the martial archer. As it was developed and had increased in effectiveness, however, it evolved into an offensive art as well, a bushido practice of one of the traditional kyudo ryu, or schools. I practiced daily, alone and as a member of a tight fraternity of other yado practitioners.*

*Even though it was against my nature, I found myself deeply involved in a combative martial art.*

*1986*

# Kentucky

I could see most of the ridge from my seat high in the crook of the tree. It was just after sunrise on a chilly November morning, and I wore a light denim jacket against the cold. In the tree for hours, I calmed myself, balancing the need to be quiet and alert against the desire to stretch. The squirrels hadn't started tromping about yet, which was good—their small leaps sounded too much like a person walking through the woods to suit me.

I could feel Luke on the next ridge and Jacob just off the trail at the fork, also quiet, also alert. They had hunted together many times and knew each other well. Bow hunting season was open from October through January, with regulations on legal game set region by region depending on the deer population. This county was legal for bucks only, which meant the deer had to be male with antlers at least four inches long.

There was what appeared to be a flint arrowhead sticking out from underneath the covering of leaves close to the base of my tree, and I made a mental note to check it when I climbed down. Arrowheads were big business here, and for good reason. This entire region had not been home to a particular tribe, but had been communal hunting grounds for many generations of many tribes. There was an abundance of artifacts, and some of the better specimens had very high price tags. I would pass the points I found through smoldering sage smoke, both to respect and also to clear their history.

I had stopped being a vegetarian a few years before, when my oldest *daughter had begun to eat solid foods, because I knew my diet was not balanced, and I wanted hers to be better. The current wisdom had been confusing on the composition of a proper vegetarian diet and called for mixing a great number of foods, most of which I felt were unappealing.*

*In return for my decision to eat meat, I made sure I hunted every fall, believing that I had responsibility for the lives of the beings that gave their lives for my family, at least symbolically. I didn't enjoy the thought of taking another being's life, but took my moral and spiritual responsibility seriously.*

*My eyes closed as I took the pulse of my surroundings, a skill learned during my years of ki practice. In deference to the spirits here I prayed for my buck, and prayed not to dishonor the proud tradition of the hunt. I also cast about to see if I could feel any beings other than my hidden friends, slowly feeling. Deer are masters, in many ways, and hide themselves well.*

*I was using a Golden Eagle compound bow, the Double Eagle model, with matched limbs and an oil painting of a Grizzly bear on the riser. Technically it was a target bow, but I preferred the smoothness of round wheels, and had covered the glossy surfaces with camouflaged material. It rested across my lap, an Easton X7 shaft in place, the Satellite broadhead ready, my gloved fingers affixed loosely to the string. Only a hundred of these bows were produced each year, all components carefully matched. My bow, which I had named Friend Stonewall, was this year's serial number twelve.*

*Hunting permission depended on a farmer's trust, and most felt better if you used a compound bow—I didn't mind. Modern compound bows appealed to me because they were easier to hold drawn, and there was very little I enjoyed as much as holding a bow at full draw. I loved my traditional equipment, that would never change, but I knew this was also archery, something to be respected.*

Snow was continuing to fall, its white blanket silencing the everyday sounds. The barn door was slid open only slightly, and I stood just inside its cover, sipping my coffee, looking down and admiring the purity of the tableau outside. I remembered an old quote to the effect that "silence contains all sounds, just as white contains all colors." It seemed appropriate.

I watched as my footprints from the house were slowly filled by the downward-floating snow. The white house, the good-smelling gray wood smoke pouring from the chimney, snow covering the now-bare trees, the bushes, the ground—it made such a vision of white-on-white that I picked up the F-1 from the workbench and took a black-and-white photograph. I wondered if there were a way to use a multi-level die to emboss an image of the scene on pure white paper, and if the image wouldn't be too subtle when it was done. I wrote the idea in my notebook, then returned to the doorway. Everything was so serene.

The silence was broken when a small blonde head poked out of the back door of the house, yelling "Daddy!," one arm waving frantically to me. I returned her wave, loving her, loving the way she loved me, then shook my head, knowing she and her little sister were probably driving their mother crazy. I slid the door shut when she disappeared back in the house, turned and contemplated my sculpture studio, still shaking my head. Little Jessica knew she wasn't supposed to bother me, so she wouldn't (theoretically) have come out to see me, but it was tough to contain that little bubble.

I practiced my yado kata, the practice dummy disguised as an archery target, then worked on Kenjitsu with the practice swords, as well as the wooden sword-shaped bokken. I then shot kyudo for an hour, bringing myself fully to my center, now ready to work.

The barn was on two levels, the earthen ramp leading to the heated top level facing the back of my house. The lower level opened in the opposite direction onto the fenced field behind the barn where the horses and other animals were kept. Smaller than the top level, it was supported by solid earth on the house side, oak posts on the field side. The dojo, or practice hall, was on the field side of the upper level and my work areas were on the earth-supported side, so the weight of my projects wouldn't strain the old structure. This building was the place that I concentrated myself, and I separated the supported part of the upper floor into two large studios, one for flat media and one for sculpture. While the inside was finished and comfortable, I chose to leave the exterior as traditional as possible, even painting it with the old red milk and rust mixture traditional to American barns.

I turned on the lights, exposing the massive marble shape to a series of bright spotlights, illuminating every detail. This set of spots purposely threw the walls and workbench into deep shadow, giving the illusion of great space, the sculpture alone against a backdrop of darkness.

Carved out of a delicately-veined piece of stone several feet high, wide, and deep, there were four small cherubs draped around a robed and bearded male figure, seated and with a large book on his lap. One cherub was hanging on and looking over the larger figure's shoulder, one was on his lap, one was to the side on tiptoe pointing at something in the book, and the fourth was leaning against his leg, pointedly ignoring the others, facing away from the group. Each had a little bow and a quiver of arrows, and the last little figure was holding his bow, fingering it absently. The larger figure, with his lined and bearded face, gave the appearance of great age and wisdom, the folds of his robe falling to the floor around the tree stump he used as a seat. Carved out of a single piece of stone, the overall effect was impressive, indeed.

After making some mental notes, I spotlighted the full-sized model that had started as several joined masses of cherry-wood, a sculpture finished months before. I was very pleased with the effect—it was so wonderful to work with warm, tight wood—when I finished a sculpture I liked to put the wooden models on a forested part of my property near one of the paths so they could be seen in a natural setting. Not only was it like a portfolio of my larger three-dimension works, but my "sculpture forest" was a popular place for my family and friends to spend time, a good place to wander.

The effect was just what I wanted in the model—it was difficult to see in the figures just who was the teacher and who the student, and all the figures were very intense (except, of course, for the cherub who was playing with his little bow). The expressions weren't yet right in the stonework, so, noting the areas that still needed work, I began.

At three o'clock, satisfied with the day's work, I walked to the house and shed my snow boots, grabbing up Jessica as I walked in the door, where she was waiting in ambush for me, hiding. No contest—her little spirit shone brightly from behind the door, revealing her hidden self to me. I hugged her, tickled her, and put her on my shoulders after I moved my braid out of the way, bouncing through the house, laughing and making silly sounds.

"Hoompa, hoompa, hoompa, here comes the Great Billy Goat Gruff! Hoompa! You better get out of the way! Hoompa!" We crashed through the kitchen, my baby's arms grasping under my chin tightly while I held on to her feet.

"Daddy Goat Gruff! Hoompa, Hoompa!" Every "Hoompa" involved a bouncy giant step, shaking the dishes in the china cabinet and the vases on their perches in the dining room. We went through the archway from the dining room into the living room, passing by the stairs leading up to our left.

"Hoompa, hoompa!" The living room shuddered under our onslaught as we circled the coffee table, stomping, stomping.

"Marcus, will you hold it down? You'll wake up Hanna! Look at what you're doing to Jessie!" Melissa was almost to the bottom of the stairs, absolutely furious, her long high ponytail whipping back and forth as she hurried.

I pulled Jessica over my head and held her out in front of me for inspection, upside down. What I saw was a wiggly, giggly, and completely happy little girl covered in white marble dust from my coveralls, her blue eyes twinkling as she squirmed, trying to right herself.

"Oops! Sorry, honey. This towhead's all messy now—do we have time to make another before dinner?" I set Jessica down, righting her, and scooped up my beautiful and angry Melissa, cradling her squirming figure like a baby in my arms, burrowing past her shirt to her belly, making a loud and wet "smurply" sound as I played her belly button like a trumpet, not stopping until she begged for mercy.

"Let me down, you oaf, now you've got me covered too—and don't step on Jessie!" Jessie, of course, had her antigravity engine going at full steam now, bouncing up and down like a little pogo stick, now running and trying to climb the stairs so she might jump on my back from the railing. I carefully put my wife down and held up my hands in defeat as Jessica came back to the bottom step.

"Sorry, Bunkin, mommy says no more. Break! Time out!"

"Sure—good luck getting her quiet now!"

"Why don't you give her some ice cream, darlin'? Let's get her really going good!"

"Yay! Ice cream!"

"No, Baby," I said. "Daddy was teasing—you know it's not time for ice cream. Why don't you give me a hug and go down to the playroom. I've got to take a shower, yes?"

"Okay, Daddy! Kiss first!" I bent down and gave her a kissy-smack on the forehead, brushing off her share of the dust from her clothes as well as I could. She bounced off to the playroom, appeased for the moment.

"You drive me nuts, do you know that? Please don't get her so hyper all the time. She takes hours to settle down—"

I had started brushing the dust off of Melissa, but my strokes were slowing down, getting more firm. "Oh, no," she said, backing away. Hanna's going to wake up any minute, and I'm still mad at you, so don't start getting any ideas! When are you going to install a shower in that barn, so we don't have to go through this every day? Do you know how hard it is to get this dust off everything?"

"Okay, okay. I'm just waiting for warmer weather, cutie, and besides, I'm going to make some other changes out there, so it's not just a matter of installing a few pipes. Nobody wants to do remodeling in this weather."

"Aren't contractors looking for something to do inside this time of year?

"Sure."

"Then why not now?"

"Well, mainly because I'm in the middle of a project, and don't want to be bothered." He thought for a moment. "You know, though, it really is going well. I think I've probably only got a week or so before I'm done, so I'll talk to Mike when he and Dina come over for supper. Is that okay?"

"Finally!"

"Hey, don't let our oldest hear you or she'll think it's playtime again."

"Okay. Why don't you take a shower, and I'll change out of these dusty things." She looked around the living room with her fists on her hips. "I guess it's not too bad in here. Damage anywhere else?"

"No, dear. We were good."

"Yeah, right. Well, come on, then."

She started up the stairs and I followed, watching her rear end as she climbed—nice. "What are you going to wear tonight?"

"I don't know, probably just jeans and a sweatshirt—Why?"

"I don't mean outside, I mean underneath." I reached up to the inside top of her denim-covered legs.

She jumped, then ran for the top of the stairs. "Now? Your shoulders don't hurt?"

"Naw, I'm just putting finishing touches on, so things aren't so physically intense, although I'd rather take a hot bath than a shower, if I've got time."

"Sure—they aren't due for a couple of hours. Let me check on the baby, okay?"

"Okay. I've got a little present for you, so hurry up." She turned left at the top of the stairs and I turned right, through our bedroom.

By the time she came in the master bathroom, I had taken my clothes off and started the water. "How's Hanna?"

"Sleeping like a baby, if you'll pardon the expression."

"Good."

"Did I hear something about a present?" She leaned back against the vanity, crossing her arms, a smile on her beautiful oval face, blue eyes twinkling.

I tested the water with my hand, wiped it off on the bath towel, winked and said "There are presents and then there are presents."

I kissed her while rubbing her slowly, then kneeled, pulling her tight jeans all the way down, admiring her beautiful belly on the way. "I know we don't have much time."

She cooperated by moving forward and grabbing the edge of the vanity with both hands.

I knew how much she loved this, so sometimes I loved it too.

When done I stood up and kissed her, a series of gentle, small, soft kisses.

"I love you, I said."

*Truth.*


Mike and Dina arrived about dark, bringing Tracey, their own little four year-old bundle of energy. They had both grown up in this area, married young, and had stayed here. Mike was a contractor and handyman with a good reputation, and Dina cared for Tracey and their home. They were good people, as kind as the day was long, and their ki didn't grate on me the way some people's did. My girls loved Tracey, though Hanna couldn't do much but crawl after her.

The older girls took Hanna off to the playroom after supper to use her as a dress-up doll, allowing the adults space for a few minutes of conversation in the firelit living room—Mike over a beer, the rest of us over coffee.

Mike's long hair and beard were both a deep brown, his hair falling around the shoulders of his blue flannel shirt, his brown eyes twinkling amidst a sea of follicles. He leaned himself back in the corner of the couch, propping his feet up on the rough-hewn coffee table, full of himself.

I sat cross-legged on the floor across the other end of the coffee table in front of Melissa's chair, tamping my favorite pipe full of Ebon-Knight tobacco. Dina sat on the other end of the couch from her husband, across from me, comfortable in her jeans, her mother's ears listening for any out of place sound.

"So," he said, "how's the sculpture coming, Marcus?" He drank from his beer, then set it down on the coaster on the end table.

"Great! It should only take a few more days to finish, then it's off to posterity." I liked Mike, and I liked his wife and child. They were honest, open people who enjoyed sharing my family's company.

"Who's buying this one?"

"I don't know if it's sold yet. You'll have to ask my agent."

"Well, agent?"

"A collector from Seattle, just today," Melissa said, leaning forward to rub my shoulders. "This is his third one. He said he was planning to give this one to the museum there, but I know this guy, and I think he'll change his mind when he sees it. It's gorgeous."

"Glad you like it, m'dear."

"When can we see it, Marcus?" Dina asked.

"Just as soon as it's done, no problem. I think it's working out very well."

Dina furrowed her brow. "Don't you ever worry about the chisel slipping at the last moment, crumbling the whole piece—like in the movies?"

"Oh, no, Dina," I explained. "You see, stone has a grain to it, like wood, but finer and denser, not to mention tougher. You just have to make sure you understand what it's going to do when you hit it, and then you hit it ex-act-ly right.

"In fact, that's why there are places famous for their marble, because the color and consistency are so even. That's one of the reasons the stuff costs so much.

"Oh, Mike," I continued. "Speaking of 'costing so much,' I need to have some remodeling-type work done on the barn when this piece is finished. How's your schedule these days?"

"I've got a bathroom I'm doing now and two kitchens waiting in line, but I can put off the first kitchen for a week or so, if you don't need anything very extensive. What do you want to do?" Mike did quality work, probably because he enjoyed it so much. He could have made much more money working in a city, but wasn't interested.

"Oh, I need a shower put in the wash area in the barn, and I want to partition part of the painting studio and put in a vent and some outlets."

"Cool. What are you going to do in the new room?"

"I, my friend, am going to start making arrows."

"You need a whole room just for arrows? Aluminum?" A loud pop came from the fireplace, throwing a spark up against the back of the screen. I reached up and turned the lamp down to a lower setting, so we could concentrate more on the fire.

"No, cedar. I haven't been very happy with the arrows I've been getting lately, and want to experiment some. No biggie, but the coatings and paints smell, so I want to put them away from everything else with plenty of ventilation. I'd also like to study some of the ways that cultures famous for archery decorated and fletched their shafts, but that's in the future. Right now I just want to play with the possibilities. Can you come over this weekend to draw up some plans for an estimate?"

"Sure. Hey, did the Japanese decorate their arrows that way?"

"No, no. Their arrows are very simple and elegant." I thought for a moment. "They use bamboo for the most part, although I have some specialty shafts made from wood. I'm afraid the problem with making their type of arrows is the exotic nature of the materials they use—the feathers, the nocks, the tips, everything is made from very cool stuff."

"How long were you there?" His beer was done.

"Six years—a long time. I still go back two or three times a year for shows, or to visit when I can, so I can get some of the materials I need. I'm still pretty close to some great people there."

"Wow, long time. Why did you come back? I mean, I know how much you loved it, and six years is a long time."

"I know, Mike, I know—a long time. No big mystery, I just got homesick, I guess. Things are intense there, not just sometimes but every single day. When I came home for a visit in '79 I realized how much I missed it, so I started spending more time here and less there."

"What about the things you were studying? Did your teachers get pissed?"

"Oh, no. I still study when I visit, so that's no problem. They know my training is so deep inside that I couldn't quit, even if I wanted to." I looked up at the display of three swords on the wall, my grandfather's saber above the long and short Japanese blades.

I explained to him that I had felt more like a kid who was going back home after finishing college than an adult changing countries. I had gotten the feeling my teachers weren't surprised, knowing I would leave someday—it had been time for me to solidify my gaijin life, to realize my adulthood. I didn't mention my deeper training or yado, of course, something my wife didn't even know existed. She often watched my kyudo or sword practice, but I had plenty of private time to study, and my learning continued and deepened on my return visits.

"Of course when I met sweety-pie Melissa here, everything changed for me, and this is home now."

"Aaw, isn't that sweet..." Mike ducked the pillow I threw, laughing.

"Mike!" Dina said. "Stop it—it is sweet; sweeter than anything you ever say about me! How did y'all meet, anyway?" She put her hands up as Mike tossed the pillow at her.

"Toss me the pillow, please, Dina," Melissa said. "These guys—When will they ever grow up?"

"I don't know, Melissa," Dina said, tossing the pillow carefully. "And sometimes I think it's a lost cause to even hope they ever will. But seriously, how did y'all meet?"

"His old agent was my boss in San Francisco, and I met him there," Melissa said, "but he was so shy I had to practically grab him by the ankles—weren't you, dear."

"Ha! It was the old 'pull away-come closer' trick... works every time!"

"Yeah—Right!" I got the pillow against the back of my head.

"So," Mike said, "you stole your boss's client, eh? Pretty sneaky."

"No, that just developed naturally—this makes more sense, anyway, don't you think?"

"It's okay by me," Mike said. "Like it's any of my business. But do you really like Backwater, Kentucky, better than San Francisco?"

"Backwater, indeed, Mike." Melissa explained that we were close enough to Danville, a college town, where the teachers are great—most were highly-educated faculty spouses, so the level of public school education was better that many private schools in other places, important now that Jessie was almost ready for school. We wanted the best of both worlds, and were only an hour or so south of Lexington, a large-enough city.

She continued, "I'm from Ohio originally, and just moved to California for the better job market, and because I had a sister out there. I was glad to move back to this side of the country. Now I can see my folks anytime I want.

"Could you imagine knowing about this place and picking to live in a city, instead?"

"Not me," Mike said.

"Me neither," said I.

"Never," Dina agreed.

"Anyway, I was the one who was really handling things for his account, so I knew his work and the client list better than the boss did. When he was in town it was natural for us to spend time together.

"Art is an amazing field, and there are people all over the world who want his work, so since we've been married I've been able to work from home and we can live wherever we want."

"Did you study art, too?" Dina asked.

"Nothing official, just some on my own. I practically grew up in museums, and really love to be around when this big dummy creates his pieces."

"Hey!" I said.

"Don't 'hey' me, buster, you know I love you, but you also know it's frustrating to try to talk to you about your work."

"You try spending some time in a place where you have to explain why you do every little thing you do. It's enough to drive you nuts, having to justify your subject matter, your brush choices, everything—it's enough to cause 'painter's block.' I don't know why I do, but I just get bored talking about a piece, analyzing it. I guess maybe I'm happiest when I actually am doing the work, and when I'm done, I'm done. Time to move on.

"Sometimes, when I really like something I've done, I can walk by it and I have to stop and look for a minute. It just fits, somehow—everything works right."

"Do you guys know much about art?" Melissa asked.

"No," Mike said. "But I really enjoy walking in the sculpture garden. I just can't believe how long it takes to make those things—and then to let those wood pieces just sit out in the weather."

"I know," I said. The room was filling with the tendrils of vanilla-tobacco smoke from my pipe, a homey smell. "But watching the wood sculptures weather and change is an important part of the process for me, too."

"Well, I'm glad you like to do the smaller projects, too," Melissa said,

"It all sells, so I don't care what you do."

"Now there is a nice attitude. Pretty damn mercenary, if you ask me." I leaned back against her legs.

"Nobody asked you," Melissa continued. "No, Mike, great art has to go beyond just being good at a technique. There has to be a sense of composition, too, and there has to be something that really speaks to you, way down deep. Some artists have it and some don't, but it seems to come so naturally to this guy that it makes me sick sometimes."

"Thank you, dear. It's nice to know you think what I do is 'great art.'"

I got the pillow on the back of my head again. "You're welcome. I know it's not 'great art' to you, but it's pretty special to us peasants."

"You don't think what you do is good, Marcus?" Mike asked.

"I didn't say that, Mike. It's sort of like an itch I have to scratch, you know? I can't take a break for more than a few days—I get antsy. I think I'm happiest when I'm working on a few things at once, and I wouldn't ever sell anything I didn't think was good.

"It doesn't have to be just the big stuff either. I started a series of posters printed by a big press in Cleveland, using different offset techniques, and I limited the edition to one thousand. It's kind of experimental stuff, but when it works it's great. The first one just delivered yesterday. It's a seascape photograph printed big—36 by 25 inches—and the cool thing is that the screen dots are very coarse and it's printed on a soft, textured paper. The overall effect is like a watercolor, and it was cheap enough to produce that I can sell them for about twenty bucks each. We'll give you one before you leave, if you want one."

"Are you going to do others?"

"Sure. I've already got ideas for a few more. The creative technical part is getting the idea across to the pressman, you know, exactly what you're trying to do. The mechanical part is easy, just a large keyline board with the dimensions and type put down, along with a slide, if it's a photograph. The toughest part of the whole thing for me though is signing and numbering each one. I keep a notebook of ideas, so the actual work doesn't take very long—it's actually almost like a break for me, especially from the sculptures."

"Melissa," Mike said, "if y'all are going to give us one, could you keep track of the number, so we can get the same number on the others?"

"Sure, Mike. See how easy it is to become a collector?" She laughed.

"Refills?"

We were all empty, so she and Dina popped out to the kitchen to get drinks, all coffee this time. When they came back, Mike and I were discussing the details of the work I wanted him to do, and I was adding a couple of logs to the fire, so they left the drinks and went to check on the girls. They were back in a few minutes, Dina carrying Tracey, Melissa cradling Hanna, and Jessica bouncing up in the rear, but with a bounce that was definitely slowed.

The ladies returned to their places, Tracey already asleep in Dina's arms and Melissa preparing to nurse Hanna. I sat back down in front of my wife and leaned back again. Jessica plopped down in my lap, snuggling.

"Well, Mike said, "I guess we'll have to go soon. These little ladies look pretty whipped to me."

"No, no!" Jessica protested, bouncing again. "Can't Tracey spend the night?" Hanna squirmed, gurgling.

"Jessie, look at her, she's already asleep! How could you have any fun if she spent the night tonight? Why don't we wait until this weekend, okay? That is, if it's okay with her parents." Melissa looked over to Dina.

"Hey, Jessie," Mike said. I'm sure we can work something out, so don't worry, okay? Why don't you just hang on to your daddy for a little while?"

"Okay." Plump. Reposition. Hug. Squirm. Relax. Quiet. Sleep. She was getting so big. She didn't fit all the way on my lap anymore, her longer legs hanging onto the floor.

We all sat quietly for a few minutes, enjoying the crackle and warmth of the fire, drinking our drinks, Hanna making the most noise with hers.

In the process of our friends' leavetaking, a sleeping Hanna was moved to the couch while I carried a very floppy Jessica up to her bed. I made sure she was comfortable, brushed my teeth, got the buffalo robe, then came back downstairs put the robe down in front of the fire, then turned off the lamp.

We made our good-byes, then came back in the house. Melissa fixed the brandy while I checked little Hanna's position. She was tucked in the corner of the couch on her little blanket, parallel to the arm with her head towards the back, content. I pulled out the middle cushion and set it next to her so she couldn't roll far, then sat on the long-haired robe, feeling the warmth of the fire, poking it absently.

My baby came in with the brandies, handing them both to me. She got the bolster and set it down along the back of the robe, then sat down next to me, close. We rested back against the thick pillow and I handed her the drink. We snuggled, swirled, and sipped, close, not saying anything for a few moments.

"Great meal tonight, Missy." I said, using my private name for her.

"Thanks. I know how much you like my lasagna. It was good, wasn't it?"

"Wonderful, but I'm still stuffed. You sure make it hard to keep my girlish figure."

"You could practice hatha yoga with me when the girls take their naps in the afternoon. I don't see why you don't do it anyway."

"You don't think I get enough exercise?"

"I didn't say that, did I? It'll keep you flexible, though."

"I haven't done that in years—maybe I will sometime. You know," I said, "before I left for Japan, it seemed as though we all studied things like that."

"A lot of people did, back then. Not many kept up with it, though." She sipped her drink.

"That's my point. We marched about things, we studied yoga, we learned how to weave, we cared about racial issues, women's issues, freedom of speech, the war, a broad range of things—and there were communes everywhere you looked! When I came back from overseas it seemed like everyone had cut their hair, got real jobs, and lived in the same kind of ticky-tacky houses we used to laugh at—everything had changed. Nobody cared about anything but making money. What happened?"

"Where have all the flowers gone, eh?"

"No, really. What changed? It was like I came back to a different country. You know, turned left at the wrong place or something."

"I'm not sure what happened—but you have to remember I was only fifteen when you left to go to Japan."

"Oh yeah—I do forget your age sometimes, don't I? Oh, well."

"You cradle robber, you."

"Me?"

"Yes, you."

"You're lucky. You missed a lot—and a lot of it wasn't much fun, either.

"It all started off so slowly and innocently, just people caring for people and trying to make things better. We thought we were doing the right thing...

"My parents brought me up as a Christian, a Presbyterian. To them it was very important for me to respect other people, but they just couldn't understand when their children included people of other colors or religions in their lives—it just didn't make sense to them.

"I used to go to a restaurant with dad, a place where he was known very well. We used to go in the back way, through the kitchen, because it was closer to the parking lot. Well, right inside the back door was a little area for blacks to eat, sort of a lunch counter type of thing, and I couldn't see them eating there time after time without it registering that these people weren't allowed to eat with us, and it didn't make much sense to me, especially since I would chat with them and talk to them whenever we came in to eat.

"I liked it better back there, I guess. Out front the waitress would make fun of my hair, which is something that always made dad uncomfortable. It always seemed so ludicrous, because this waitress had a bleached-blonde beehive hairdo that always made me want to laugh." I looked at the fire, feeling the flames light up my face, and, in my reverie, it was if I was back there again.

"Did I ever tell you why I left Boy Scouts?"

"No. I just assumed you reached the age limit. I know it was important to you."

"Very important. I came up through Cub Scouts, Boy Scouts, and then Explorers, earning merit badges and rankings, going on three or four trips a year. I almost reached the cutoff age, but not quite. There was a new kid that moved in to the area who was black. He was a really nice guy who had been very active in scouting in his old neighborhood. That was a time of great change for everyone, you know, integrating the schools and everything. It always tickled me, because it seemed as though it was the people in the big northern cities who were talking down to us Southerners about the need to integrate, and then they found out the truth—that you Yankees were as segregated as we were."

"Me. A Yankee?"

"Still a very important point to a Southerner, but I love you anyway. My mother still calls the Civil War the 'War of Northern Aggression,' you know.

"The main difference between the north and the south in the '60's was that our neighborhoods were close to each other and yours were far apart, so when everyone was required to integrate, it meant many times we had to stop bussing, and you had to start—that tickled me.

"Anyway, I invited this guy, Jerry, to join our Explorer Post and was surprised when he told me that I'd better check with my leaders before I invited him. I was even more surprised when they said no—no discussion, no nothing, just no.

"I was the vice-president and my girlfriend was the mascot, but I walked out that night, and I've never seen any of those men again—Adults that had practically raised me from the time I was eleven years old. It really shocked me."

"Girlfriend, huh?"

"Long-gone, m'dear. Long gone. A cutie, though..." I got a pinch on my thigh.

"Hey!"

"Hey, yourself!"

"Anyway, that turned out to be the start of things, especially with Nixon and Agnew in office. By the time I graduated from high school in '69 it seemed like one or the other of them were on TV every night telling the world how bad we were, how evil those were who wanted to change things. Those next few years weren't great for us, especially below the Mason-Dixon line. We were definitely in the minority, that's for sure, and had to be careful about exposing ourselves too much.

"I remember being stopped by a cop for a traffic ticket just before I left for Japan, and the guy was actually pleasant to me, so I talked to him for a few minutes. During the late '60's and early 70's I was stopped by the police quite often, usually while driving, so it wasn't a new situation for me, but I wasn't used to a friendly attitude. I asked him what had changed so drastically, and he knew exactly what I meant—no pussyfooting or evasion.

"He said that when they arrested someone and put them in jail that the first thing they did was to cut the prisoner's hair—and he didn't think he had to worry about me because he could tell from the length of my hair that I couldn't have been in jail for years! I was flabbergasted. I asked him why somebody hadn't thought of that before, but he didn't seem to have an answer.

"I guess that's when things turned around, after Nixon and Agnew were gone. They were such vindictive people, so hateful—and they had so much power."

"Ah, the good old days."

I set my glass down on the floor behind the bolster.

She set hers down as well.

I put my arm around her. "Do you know why I'm left-handed sexually?"

"What?"

"You did know that, didn't you?"

"I hadn't really thought about it before—I didn't even know there was such a thing."

"Sure there is." I unbuttoned the top two buttons of her blouse with my left hand, slowly, lightly and warmly touching her firm skin as I went, down between her breasts, then back up the side of her neck to the space behind her right ear. Her eyes closed as my hand went back down to the next button, then up again, then down, then up. By the time I had her shirt completely open, she was purring. I went farther.

"Hey!" she said.

"I like this game."

"Might I remind you that I'm the one with all the ammunition, sir? You don't stand much of a chance of winning, now do you?"

"Who said I wanted to win?"

"Ah!"

"Before you go too far why don't you check on Jessie? We don't want any little eyes peeking around, you know."

"Okee-Doke!" I popped up, took the glasses to the kitchen, then went upstairs to check on my older bunkin. She was completely out, holding her little Ernie doll. I pulled the blanket over her and snuck out, first to get a warm washcloth, then back downstairs.

Hanna had been shifted and covered, so I knew Missy had checked her. I took off my shirt as I walked across the living room.

Melissa, her shirt re-buttoned, smiled at me as I laid on my stomach.

She started rubbing my shoulders. Wonderful. I stretched my arms up above my head, so she could manipulate each muscle, kneading them one by one, releasing the tension. I guessed it had been a rougher day than I thought.

She moved down my back, deeply squeezing the muscles down either side of my spine, relaxing me. She took her strong thumbs and pressed them down hard to penetrate the firm muscles of my shoulders, relaxing me even more.

She continued down my legs, doing each thigh, then each calf—they had been especially sore lately. She spent several minutes on my rock-hard feet, travelers of the earth.

She had me turn over and worked her expert hands up the tops of my feet, my shins, my thighs. My baby knew what to do to me, and I tried to envelop myself in every moment.

When she was done she rolled of onto her back and held up her arms to me, inviting me to lie with her. I joined her, giving her gentle kisses on her mouth and neck, feeling her shiver when I stimulated a sensitive spot. I relaxed and situated her so we were both lying on our backs, her head cradled on my shoulder, my arm around her.

This woman. I've had my share of relationships, of course, being reasonably attractive and growing up in the "frisky sixties," but I had never felt this way about anyone. We fit together so well...

The first time I put my arm around her something grabbed me and had never let me go. It felt like I wanted to envelop her, to wrap her up within me, to hold her all over, all at once. I couldn't get enough of her, and counted myself so very blessed.

I was the most surprised, I think, when I realized just how deeply I had fallen for this lady. I remembered the day, when, waiting for someone on a street corner, I saw an attractive woman walking toward me on the sidewalk, and my very first thought was: How wonderful my Melissa would look in that outfit. Instead of assessing this stranger's beauty or appeal, I wondered only how sexy my own sweetheart would look in that same outfit, how her graceful walk would improve the lines of the dress, how it would set off her figure, how my baby's coloring would improve the gestalt.

I kissed her forehead, gently, rousing her from her own little reverie, and we started to get ready to go upstairs. As she stood up she stopped. "Hey," she said, "what were you starting to say about sexual left-handedness?" She moved over to her chair where she had put her clothes.

"Oh, that. A theory of mine, I guess.

"In high school the only place I could be alone with a girlfriend was in the car, you know? So, assuming I was the driver, that meant when we parked that it was my left hand that was best situated to feel around, and after I became pretty good at feeling around, it was most natural to do it with my left hand."

I wasn't expecting the pillow this time, and it almost knocked me over.

*I stood on the indoor shooting line with nineteen other shooters, in marked lanes two feet wide. There were several different classes represented, from the bowhunting traditional recurve and longbow shooters to the highest-tech compounds. There were twenty others waiting their turn—our line shot the top row of targets, theirs the lower, all arranged against an extremely well-lit rank of tightly-bound cardboard squares two feet thick, twenty yards distant.*

*I didn't mind coming to Ohio for these shoots, because there was such an intensity in these competitors. One of the reasons I loved shooting with these people was the way they would always give advice to another archer—even a competitor. It seemed to typify the Spirit of Archery.*

*I was shooting Target Release AA, the most mechanized class, which meant it also had the highest scoring requirements. My new target compound had a custom ten-power scope mounted on the front, balanced by a micro peep sight in the string—between the two I had a very tight view of the inner four, five, and x-rings. The entire target was eighteen inches across, but there was usually no way to win a competition at this level if even one shaft landed outside the five ring.*

*The x-ring was a little larger than one and one-half inches in diameter inside the five-ring, which was about twice that size. The highest possible score for one shot was a five with an x, with five shots to an end, four ends to a game, and three games to a round—so the highest score possible was three hundred with sixty x-rings. Most shooters at this level used a "five-spot" target; a single target with five smaller targets, one in each corner, one in the middle, with each small target consisting of only the four, five, and x-rings. For each end, then, there would be one arrow in each target.*

*This bow had a sixty-five percent letoff, which meant at full draw I was only holding twenty-one pounds instead of the entire sixty pounds the bow generated—my beloved Double Eagle had only a thirty-five percent letoff, which was good for fingers, not so good for release, because a clean shot without a release mechanism needed some weight to pull against the fingers.*

*I preferred a single-spot, the full-sized target. I used Easton A/C shafts, the Aluminum/Carbon high tech shafts that were fairly new on the market. Each shaft was absolutely matched to the others. The tips used the PWS—the Point Weight System—and had to be custom weighted for each shaft so the balance point fell between the actual center of the shaft and the raw balance point—a lot of work, delicate work. I used tiny black feather fletch on the shafts, only 2 1/4" long and 1/2" tall, both for* the reduced wind resistance and so the fletch wouldn't interfere with the other arrows in the target.

One of the major keys to a perfect shot is to aim at the smallest point possible, so I mentally split the x-ring into its own little five-spot. When your arrows are only 1/4" wide, there are acres of space in that x-ring, and the area of concentration gets absolutely tiny.

I had shot the two warm-up ends, five arrows each, and micro-adjusted the scope just the tiniest fraction, more as a mental check than a physical one. We were now waiting for the match to begin, each shot critical. I held the bow horizontally to my body, the top of the bow towards the target and the weighted tip of the thirty-six inch stabilizer resting on the ground, holding the bow's weight.

When the rangemaster gave the official starting signal I raised the bow, took a deep, centering breath, and closed my eyes—there were a full five minutes allowed to shoot the five arrows, no hurry. I pulled the first arrow out of the full-sized hip quiver, noting its number, then attached it to the string, cocking the Barner rest to hold the arrow. When I released the arrow, the spring-loaded rest would fall out of the way, allowing the arrow to pass without any contact. I attached the hair-trigger mechanical release, a pincer design I had found to be absolutely stable.

I raised the bow, holding my left arm horizontal, twisting my elbow so its hollow part faced the bow—it was a minor point, but it allowed the string to pass my arm with a fraction of an inch to spare— it meant I didn't need an armguard for protection. The grip had a flattened back that allowed a straight hand position, so elbow position was critical. I named this bow Sensei Talon, a name to honor the eagle.

I smoothly pulled the string with the wrist strap of the Overkill release, keeping my fingers well away from the trigger, inhaling as I drew, feeling the increase in weight, then the letoff. When the mechanical draw stops on the cables met, everything stopped firmly, and I pulled my hand all the way into the bottom of my jaw, resting my thumb around the back of my neck, slowly and slightly exhaling. It was important for everything to be absolutely stable and absolutely consistent, so there were a hundred little things I did to make sure this shot would be the same as each other.

I stood at full draw, the bowstring crossing at the corner of my mouth—I could feel it there under my moustache. The peep sight was positioned correctly in front of my right eye, my dominant eye, and I lined up the small dot of the single-element scope with a place just inside the lower left circle of the x-ring—my number one position for my number one shaft. I drew

*smooth half-breaths, keeping everything very stable, noting that there was
no sway in the stabilizer sticking out so far in front of the bow.*

*I delicately placed my second finger so it rested lightly on the front of
the trigger, and made sure my bow hand rested the way it was supposed
to on the grip, positioned well but relaxed, pushing to the right place,
everything in me cooperating to send the arrow properly to the target, my
left elbow pointing straight back. I held the position, feeling the connection
with my targeted spot.*

*I let my finger gently rest on the trigger, releasing the string, making
sure no other part of either hand moved at all while keeping my form firm,
then watched the arrow as it flew cleanly towards its home. I held my
shooting position until the arrow hit the target, exhaling as it flew.*

I'd made omelettes for breakfast—one of my specialties. I enjoyed the
entire process, but especially cutting the mushrooms. Somehow I got a
kick out of making each equal slice with a clean cut, using the thin-bladed
knife to make a staggered pile. It was always a challenge for me to have
the omelettes and the toast ready at the same time, but it was a challenge
I accepted—and today it had worked.

We ate in the kitchen, then cleaned things up. Melissa went to help
Jessica gather a few last things, took them outside to to the RV, then came
back inside.

"Are we ready to go yet?" I asked.

She had spent the weekend getting the rented Winnebago ready for
the trip to Seattle, but was visibly edgy for some reason. I was holding
Hanna and had shifted my braid around so she could pull on it—her favorite
thing to do, I think because she could get my attention anytime she wished.
She was walking now, and attempting to drive us both to distraction.

"No, dear, we're still waiting for the driver." The marble sculpture had
been loaded into the big van yesterday, and we were going to follow it all
the way through to final delivery and setup. We enjoyed these trips.

A project this size created its own set of problems. The client had
flown out here, seen (and loved) the project and returned home with the
specs and photographs, so he could find a home for the marble behemoth.
I liked the guy—he was genuinely nice. It had taken him so long to find the
proper place that by the time he had just the spot he wanted, not only had
the work on my barn been completed, but spring had come as well.

As soon as the driver got here, we would start another odyssey, trekking across the Midwest all the way to the west coast, staying until the piece was properly installed. We would return along the southern route, taking a few weeks to enjoy the southwestern spring. The toughest thing about these trips was making sure everything was taken care of—our home and all our pets. Mike's brother was going to watch everything, and I had spent my day yesterday making sure he understood everything. I was ready, too, but it seemed as though Missy was especially anxious.

"What's going on, baby? Is anything wrong?" She was the only one that really understood the network of people and galleries an agent has to know, and I thought perhaps she was upset about something business-related, for a trip like this was important for exposure—there were even television interviews set up in Seattle.

"No, no, I'm just afraid I've forgotten something, that's all."

"How? I think everything we own is in that RV."

"Cute. Real cute."

"You realize, of course, that once Jessica starts school in the fall we won't be able to do this kind of thing together for a long, long time." We loved these trips, and I knew she would miss them. To my surprise she started crying—crying real tears.

"Baby! What's wrong?" I put Hanna down in her playpen and went to hold her.

"I didn't want to tell you yet, but it's going to be longer than you think." I didn't see her upset that often, and was deeply concerned.

"What? What do you mean?"

"Oh, Marcus, I'm pregnant again."

My heart skipped a beat. "Are you okay?"

"Sure I am—Oh! No, no. I'm not upset because I'm physically not-okay. I'm upset because this means it's going to be even longer before we're kid-free."

"Pardon?"

"You know—all the traveling we had talked about once the kids were grown up and gone. Now it's going to be even longer before we can live like that."

"And that's what's bothering you."

"Sure, doesn't it bother you?"

"Baby, I think we make beautiful babies together—I love our kids and I love you, and I also know we're going to be together a long time. When the kids grow up, then we'll deal with the things we want to do—my gosh, look around you—does it look like we're deprived? Don't you know how wonderful our life is?"

"Of course I do, Marcus, but I thought—"

"Listen," I interrupted. "Don't you want this baby?"

"More than anything!"

"And aren't we okay with money?"

"Of course!"

"Then aren't we okay—better than okay?"

"Sure, but... Oh, I don't know! Sometimes I guess I feel so lonely out here in the country—and to have another baby, too?"

I got some rich-smelling coffee and walked to the back door, looking out at the barn beyond the RV and the big enclosed van. "Do you want to hire someone to help? A nanny, maybe?"

"Oh. Marcus, I don't know what I want. Extra help would be nice, but I like the freedom we have here on our own—I don't want to bring in a stranger."

"I know, I know. What are our options?"

"God, I don't know."

"Would you like your mother to come and visit for awhile—just the time around the birth?"

"Maybe, I don't know. We can talk about it on the trip, I guess."

"Sure—we certainly have enough time for it. Listen, I need to close out the Macintosh and move it to the RV, so I should do that now. Do you need anything from the IBM?"

"No, I've got everything I need for the trip copied to the new HP laptop. I hate working with that small LCD screen, but it'll be good to have it on the trip. It was such a good present, sweetie. Thank you."

"You're welcome, Missy. I'm still waiting for a battery-operated Mac, so I can do my graphic stuff away from the office."

"Is the new software okay?"

"Sure, and it'll be fun to play with on the trip—I just wish it didn't draw so much current."

"You'll be okay—between driving and the kids there'll be plenty to do."

"Oh, I know—just wishful thinking."

*Just twenty yards away from the back porch towards the woods there is a circle of sand, twenty-eight feet in diameter. Stacked to a height of eighteen inches around it, like a low wall, is a border of seasoned firewood with an opening that faces the East.*

*The Center of the circle is another circle, about eight feet in diameter, surrounded by a ring of foot-thick stumps laying on their sides. The sand in it is blackened and mixed with the ashes from many fires.*

*There are large logs and rude wooden chairs surrounding the fire-place, settled into well-used positions.*

*Many evenings around dark I would enter this Circle, bowing as I entered, then walking in the proper direction, like it was the inside of a tepee. After lighting the fire I would sit there for hours, sometimes thinking about things, sometimes talking with family or friends, sometimes just staring into the entrancing flames.*

*It had become a special place to me over the years, a Holy Place. I had started something new last summer that I liked to do once a week now; I would be out here at dawn and mark a point at the edge of the circle showing where the sun had risen that day.*

*As I gathered the markers, it was beginning to feel like I had my own little Stonehenge or Great Pyramid. I felt like I was starting to connect to this place as more than just a house and some land, as important as that was to have, and even more than a home, as crucial as that was to a family.*

*1992*

# Ohio-Pennsylvania

*I picked the newly-crested arrow out of the drying rack, inspected it for quality, then held it up to the Graybark for comparison.*

*Black Widow Bows made a special-edition Diamond Anniversary series of bows from 1987 through '90. The Crown Jewel model had the target recurve's traditional reddish-orange finish with a logo-scrimshawed ivory medallion set in the handle. The Graybark, however, had a gray finish, using a stain that muted the color of the wood while allowing the beautiful grain to show through. It was accented with two reddish-orange stripes inlaid vertically through the riser, one about 3/8" of an inch wide, the other only about 1/8", and the wider inlay was accented with a black and a white stripe. I had ordered mine with an all-black string, and it had delivered with an orange serving, the strong thread-like material wrapped around the center of the string to protect it from wear. I asked for a sixty-four inch bow with a forty-six pound draw at twenty-nine inches, and that is exactly what she measures. I named this bow Sensei GreyBeard, and it's true to its name, teaching me every time I shoot.*

*Shooting a bow on an outdoor field range presents a special set of challenges, including shooting at unknown yardages, having to twist into unusual shooting positions dictated by terrain, and dealing with the feisty wind. The basics, though, seem as though they would get old after a while—after all, it is primarily the same act endlessly repeated. The truth is, though, there are so many nuances to shooting that archery never grows old, and is truly the lifetime teacher the Japanese consider it to be.*

*Archery to me embodied analogies of many life lessons, primarily dealing with attitude. In western archery my goal would be to reduce the overall diameter and position of my group of shots, and the more sensitive I was to my shooting style the easier it was to determine a technical growth path. In kyudo, however, even though hitting the target in the center was the desired result, the position of the shot was deemed only to be a reflection of the archer's inner state. The proper attitude was seen to be of vital importance, at least after basic technique was firmly established, and it was considered a basic truth that body, mind, and spirit were closely interrelated and dependent on one another for a proper result. I was lucky to have both traditions, to be able to pay attention to the inner and the outer in any style of shooting.*

*One of the things I learned from archery that extended to my daily life was that it seemed always necessary to pay very close attention to the effects of my actions and to learn, really learn, from diligently practicing something important to me. I also learned that it was important to pay attention to the things that seemed insignificant to me, that if I didn't recognize them as important, they would return as larger issues in the future. I don't think this was any more critical than in the practice of developing and maintaining a committed relationship.*

*I knew how blessed I was to have a woman sensitive enough to be considerate of my needs, connected enough to really respond to my caresses, and free enough to allow herself to actively respond to me. My life-partner is warm, intelligent, tasteful, attractive, and responsive—we never tire of each other. This is evident even in those intimate moments we make love to each other, even though it is basically the same act endlessly repeated.*

*There is something we know as the Archer's Paradox. When an arrow is released, the immediate force on the back of the shaft causes it to push quickly against the weighted front, bending around the bow in the direction it is released (to the left of the bow when released by fingers of the right hand, because the fingers release to the left; to the right of the bow when released by a Japanese glove or by an oriental thumb-ring, because they release to the right). It is important for the arrow to flex just the right amount—too much and it won't "straighten up and fly right," too little and the shaft will hit the bow as it passes, making the arrow veer off course. The flexibility of the arrow is called the "spine weight," and it directly relates to the bow's draw weight and the archer's shooting style, especially with wood or aluminum arrows.*

*My baby had the perfect spine weight for me, and mine was perfect for her.*

Leaning back against the tree, I crossed my legs and put the Macintosh PowerBook 170 on my lap, opening the cover and bringing the little laptop out of sleep mode. The page layout file was waiting for me, just as I had left it.

I reviewed the catalogue pages visually as thumbnails, made a few minor changes, then quit, saving the file as I left. I put it back to sleep and closed the cover, setting it beside me in the grass. I would transfer the updated file to the main desktop unit, the IIci, when I went back home. I settled back to relax a few minutes out here in the yard, and considered taking a walk down by the creek before everyone got back from town—I had time.

We were full into summer now, visiting Melissa's parents at their place in northern Ohio for a few weeks. As a compromise to help Melissa with her isolation, we had settled into a routine that involved visiting her folks for a while in the summer and mine in Florida over Christmas break. It didn't solve all of our problems, but it helped, and we finally bought an RV of our own. That let us travel to other places, including various traditional shoots around the country—mostly up and down the east coast, even up into Ontario.

Jessica was ten now, going into the fifth grade this year, Hanna was to be in second, little Markie in first, while baby Samantha, now three, loved to go to daycare two or three times a week. We were definitely tied down during the school year, but were still able to have our moments—both as a family and alone.

My style of work had changed over the years as well. Now I did more small projects, many mass-produced, which allowed me more time in the house during the day. The computer had become a welcome tool, freeing me from home and the studio, at least for the printed projects, though I cherished my alone time as much as ever. My family and I were a team, and it felt very natural for us to be together.

The catalogue I was working on now was one we had been putting out every other year for the last few years, filled with my currently available pieces. I was grateful I had developed somewhat of a following, and that sales were brisk. The catalogue went to museums and other resellers as well as individual customers, and many outlets sold my work as well, mostly editions of the poster series. A few bucks on each sale worked quite well, thank you very much. Some things were even carried in the Smithsonian catalogue, which was a real boost.

Oddly enough, one of the best-sellers of the bunch was a hardcover book I designed and had printed in the off years, a book that was itself a catalogue—a catalogue of all the saleable work I had ever produced, along with its last-known whereabouts and owners of major pieces. The concept had excited collectors, museums—everyone, it seemed, and had upped the value of almost everything I had ever produced. I called the book *The Phenomonym*, though I wasn't sure why—I liked the word, and it somehow seemed to fit. It had turned into its own phenomenon, and I sometimes produced new works just so I could round out its contents to my liking. People from all over the world would send us the news when a piece changed hands, which took a certain amount of verification and record-keeping.

We now had a two-person office staff to handle the catalogue orders and other computerized paperwork, had added a room addition to the house with its own entrance, and kept a small warehouse in Lexington to ship things—all very tidy, all run by my Melissa, all set up to give us as much personal time as possible. I did my own computer work on the PowerBook and the IIci, a desktop that ran two color monitors—a twenty-one inch and a thirteen inch. I used a trackball and a large drawing tablet with the IIci setup, and was constantly trying to wring the best quality work out of my toys.

I was considering hiring someone to help me with the arrows I was making as well—I wasn't offering them for sale yet, but wanted to, and knew they would sell quickly. They had become something I gave as gifts, very popular gifts.

I enjoyed being the only source for them, but each individual arrow took so much time that I knew I wouldn't be able to handle the demand. I was worried about passing on my techniques, because many of the processes were original and had taken a great deal of time and research to perfect. As with many artists, though, I was loath to teach my secrets to someone else, no matter what the need.

I was one of those most-fortunate people able to make money from doing things I loved—and almost everything I came up with seemed to sell to someone.

Content, I decided to take my walk, to take a bow and some shafts with me to practice my yado kata in the woods, and perhaps even to do some random stump-shooting, what used to be called roving.

*I walked down the far side of the field, feeling the sun on my shoulders, the warm earth under my feet. There was a large ditch at the far edge, ten feet across and four deep, a special place for me this time of year.*

*The ditch was overgrown with huge bushes with tiny white flowers. There was only one place where there was a rough path through them, though the bushes almost touched, even at eye level. There were enough large trees for the sun and shade to dapple the end of the field in a continually changing pattern of open shadow and light, with a breeze that made everything wave and flow.*

*I could hear the buzzing several yards away and began walking toe-first, the quiet, slow walk that allowed me to silently glide. I was engrossed with everything I saw, and felt a part of it—the sensations of warmth, light, wind, buzzing, the sweet smells—all intermixed with me. I felt like I belonged right here, right now.*

*When I reached the bushes I watched the bees closely, lighting on one flower for a few moments then moving on to the next. I gently moved closer, careful not to alarm them. I moved quietly down the near slope of the ditch, then stopped halfway, standing still. I must have watched them purposely move about me for at least ten minutes, and laughed a quiet little when my yellowish-tan hair started to get its own visitors. They never stayed very long—nothing very sweet about my hair, I knew. They tickled when they walked across my shoulders.*

There was to be a yearly traditional shoot at the Denton Hill Ski Resort near Coudersport, Pennsylvania—a good summer use of the property—and Melissa had decided not to go, but to stay with her folks and take the kids up to Cedar Point Amusement Park for a few days—and I wished her well. Our kids were all bright and happy, as bouncy as they come, so I didn't envy her the task she had set for herself. Her mother was going to go with her to help, but trying to keep track of our four farm-raised children was like trying to keep several eight-week old puppies inside a wicker basket.

I took the RV on my own—I would get to visit the shoot for three days, she would get to spend more time with her folks. It was tough saying good-bye, as always, but the bunkins had been distracted by the promised trip at Cedar Point, and I was able to get off with a minimum of fuss.

I took 224 east to I-71, then went north to I-271 so I could bypass Cleveland and take I-90 east into Pennsylvania. Once there, I could take 17 over to Olean, then hit the back roads winding through the hills. I liked to meander on roads like that, and would always be on the lookout for interesting photographs to take—difficult to do with the children about.

I had left very early so I might have the afternoon on these roads, and once I was on them I stopped four or five times, taking black & white and color photographs with my Hasselblad, three backs and various lenses. The camera was several years old, but I liked the quality of the larger-negative photographs it yielded.

I shot some rock formations, an interesting old wooden fence, and a group of signs in Coudersport I was able to get at just the right angle.

I began looking for the Denton Hill grounds after I left town, but stopped when I saw an interesting old barn. It was nestled just inside a tree line perpendicular to the road, and difficult to see, but its size and position fit into its surroundings so interestingly that I had to investigate. The old gravel path that led to it was free of any vegetation, hard-packed with long-ago use, but everything else was overgrown.

It had not been designed to be weatherproof, with inch-wide cracks in the unpainted, gray-weathered rough board walls and many small holes in its rusty tin roof, but had a wide door that still swung freely, showing its dirt floor and plenty of cobwebs. Perhaps it had been a horse barn at one time, but there were no other structures around to give any clues. I took a few more pictures, inside and out, studying the garage-size structure surrounded by trees. I was able to get a shot I particularly liked—the sun leaking through the cracks in the wall in well-lit streams with dust motes glittering, suspended in air.

My photographs were something else that sold very well. I had worked with a mechanically-inclined friend of mine to design a frame for my eight-by-tens that allowed the purchaser to easily rotate through a selection of photographs. These frames and photos were offered in the catalog as well, singly or in sets—in fact, the photos themselves took up about a third of the catalogue.

I always remembered the things I photographed—in fact, I had trouble remembering someone's face until I had taken their photo, which was quite embarrassing at times. I supposed this was a reflection of the way I looked at people, as much with the spirit as with the eye. As I shot the photos other thoughts were triggered as well, though, feelings of spatial relationships, possible uses in future projects. As I stood in the barn, then, I was feeling how wide and long the interior space was, where the supports were, how the color of the dirt floor matched the color of the unpainted wall, how a curious little wooden-shuttered door was set in the side wall—and any or all of these things would remain a part of me, popping up at some point to give me an inspiration when I needed it.

I enjoyed photography, and thought one of the reasons it was interesting was because it "happened" in a single moment, much like a kata, and so it carried the same flow of artistic oneness as did sumi-e or kyudo for me.

When I finished I left, careful to leave no traces of my visit to this abandoned structure on its little-traveled road. I continued to the entrance of Denton Hill, which turned out to be just around the next couple of curves on the right-hand side of the road. This was Thursday, and I was told at the front gate that nothing was really scheduled to happen until tomorrow afternoon, so I followed the road down and around to the right, parked at the end of the farthest camping field, set up, and looked around, taking Sensei GreyBeard with me to one of the practice ranges set up on either side of the pine and fieldstone lodge.

Everything was arranged around hills, of course, since this was a popular skiing area in the winter, and the main slopes were just behind the lodge. The slopes meant there were precious few flat areas—basically just those used for parking and camping. The lodge itself was on two levels connected by a stairway—the dining and gathering areas on the top level, its entrance on the hillside, and the bathing and storage facilities on the lower, accessible from the parking areas. There were no overnight accommodations except for campers, and only one pay phone outside the lodge's lower level.

There were three "courses" winding up different parts of the hills that were set up for the competition. A course was a spaced series of dense foam animal-shaped targets set up at unmarked yardages, off a path marked with painted arrow-signs, each arrow pointing to the next station, sometime hundreds of yards away, the trail almost always up or down a hill.

A group of shooters (usually four) would follow a course and stop at each station in turn, shooting at the animal target. Scoring depended on where the target was hit, high score on each target given for the heart area.

Shooting at unmarked yardages, up hill and down, sometimes over ravines or across creeks—this was a challenging sport, made even more challenging by the people that set up the courses. They would sometimes set the targets in unusual positions, partially conceal them, haul them up into trees, or even set them at the near edge of a river—whatever they thought would make the course more "interesting." Sometimes it was as much of a challenge to figure out where the actual target was as it was to shoot it, and the range directors for each shoot took pride in coming up with new and unusual courses—the entire shooting community would compare different courses and different shoots through the off-season, and it was always a lively topic around the campfires at night.

One of the most interesting ploys, I thought, was when two targets were used on different parts of the course that looked the same but were vastly different in size. If you knew a bear target was six feet tall because you had shot it at station two, then when you saw that same shaped target uphill at station fifteen you would assume it was six feet tall as well. The catch, of course, was that it was now a half-sized target and your arrow would sail well over its top. Cute.

I wasn't as interested in attempting the courses as in practicing my shooting, watching others shoot, checking out the sales booths with the ever-helpful vendors, and reconnecting with friends. There would be a festival atmosphere once things got under way—special aerial shoots (for the kids as well as the adults), auctions, raffles, novelty shoots, and plenty of good-natured kibitzing.

At the practice range on the far side of the lodge I began warming up, shooting at foam targets set at various distances.

The arrows I had made for this bow suited it perfectly—the gray stain mixed with just a hint of green, the orange, black, and white accent stripes that matched those on the bow—even the positions of the accent colors were the same, so when the arrow was mounted on the string their colors blended with the bow where it crossed the riser. Every time I nocked an arrow on the string, it was obvious they were meant for one another.

There was another advantage as well—if the stripes on the arrow should ever not align with those on the bow, then I would immediately know the brace height of the bow was wrong, that if I were to shoot the arrow, it would not go where it was supposed to go.

One of the lessons of kyudo was isha isho—one shooting, one life. Every time I shot, then, the coordination of the colors of the arrow to the bow would help me reflect on this equipment, and how special each and every individual shot should be. This helped me to concentrate, to connect, to give each action the time, the grace, the honor, and the concentration it deserved. I could have nocked one arrow on the string before the first even hit the target because of my training, but wanted to savor each action, enjoy each motion.

Japanese arts forms, or at least the ones I have studied, have a hierarchy of skill levels. The most basic of these is a firm understanding of the art, a slow and deliberate repetition of each movement and stroke until it becomes second nature. Most never leave this stage, many never becoming expert at this level.

The second level is "middle form." A practitioner at this level could forego absolutely rigid structure, creating semi-spontaneous art and motion while still adhering to the basics of the art.

At the third level, mastery was unquestioned, and spontaneity was combined with speed. I was at a tea ceremony once, admiring a scroll-mounted piece of calligraphy. The lady who was performing the ceremony for me told me who had made it—a master with a great reputation. When I asked her what it said, she let me know in no uncertain terms it was much too beautiful for her to be able to read. Such was the highest form—communication was not limited to the art form itself, but reached beyond it. I still had trouble understanding this concept, but there were times that I understood, though briefly.

After an half-hour or so of practice I finished my shooting and went into the lodge to see when supper was going to be available. I had forty-five minutes, so I wandered about, looking for familiar faces.

There were going to be a couple hundred shooters here this weekend, and there were very few of us who didn't carry our bows all weekend long. Most of the time I can't carry my gear openly, except for in the woods, of course, and around my house and property. Sometimes I could get away with it in a small town, but when I did I still got the stares. I suppose the long hair and (sometimes) bare feet contributed to the stares as well, not surprisingly.

Here, though, it was like being in a small city with constant new arrivals, but it was a city of archers, and that made all the difference. We all spoke the same language, we all had things to teach and to learn. Most people here were short-hairs, but that seemed to be true no matter where I went—I never seemed to see very many men with long hair these days, a few friends excepted, though the average had grown—only some of the old timers kept to the old fifties' styles. What mattered to these people was not how you looked, though, but what you knew about your art.

I only seemed to feel completely comfortable when it was natural to carry my bow and wear a quiver, so this was heaven—the only thing better would have been to have my Melissa by my side—I thought of her as my Diana, my archer-goddess.

Here, though, not only could I remain dressed, as it were, but feel natural about it. Because of yado I always needed to have arrows close-at-hand, to be aware of where they were at all times. I practiced with many types of quivers, even designing a few, but just being able to openly wear one of them in public was special.

Today I was wearing a green handmade quiver, a single-strap over-the-shoulder quiver with both smooth and suede complimentary leathers. This was made like a tube, tapering from about four inches at the top down to just under three inches at the bottom. I carried eight target arrows, two hunting shafts, and two yado shafts—I felt ready for anything.

I found a couple of guys I knew from past shoots relaxing at their camp. They had a plastic tarp set up between an RV and some poles, giving them a covered area about twenty-five feet wide by thirty feet long, and were getting their fire going just outside the tarp's edge. They had folding chairs, a stack of neatly cut firewood, two coolers of beer, a portable stereo, a full-sized charcoal grill, and enough food for an army. They invited me to stay, and I made myself at home.

These guys were ready to party, to eat, drink, tell stories, and to have fun. I have never been much of a drinker, but I accepted a very cold dark beer from Hal. He and Walter were from the Jersey shore, connected somehow with the fishing trade, and made their own bows, as many traditional shooters did—still in the future for me.

We admired each other's bows, arrows (except for the yado shafts, of course—I deflected their curiosity about those), quivers, and shooting gloves, swapping stories of how each was made or acquired.

Hal shot an English longbow, a self-bow made from Pacific Yew. It surprises many people to learn that the best yew in the world is found in our country, since the English are the culture with the reputation as longbow shooters. The wood is difficult to get now, though, because its bark is the source for a cancer-fighting drug they haven't yet learned to synthesize. Those who want to use the wood for bows can only use the wood from the trees that have had their valuable bark gathered by medical collectors.

Selfbows are made from a single piece of wood, called a stave. The straightest staves are prized by bowyers, who lovingly shave them down to their final shape, "tillering" the limbs to bend correctly at the proper draw weight and length, a slow and careful process. The finished bow is a clean statement of simple elegance, usually with carved horn tips and a leather piece wrapped at the grip.

Walter preferred an American Longbow, a laminated design with a flatter cross-section than the English style. He had patterned his bow after one he had that was made by Monarch, a bow made with a rosewood riser and red cedar limbs, a beautiful combination.

He showed me the Monarch, sixty-four inches long with a sixty-four pound draw weight. It had been made two years ago, part of a trial by the bow company to use Red Cedar. It had gracefully carved stag reinforcements at the tips, shaped to complement the limb ends, and the rosewood riser pieces matched strikingly with the reddish limb color.

Walter didn't use this bow since he finished his own and offered it to me for a good price. It was a beautiful thing, a little heavy for me, but gorgeous nonetheless. We tried it at the practice range for a while and agreed on the sale.

Even though it was heavy, the Monarch was a fast and very quiet bow, probably the most quiet I had ever shot—important in a hunting bow. I was already thinking of what colors I would use for the arrows to match this bow as we returned to his site.

We all talked for hours, through supper and hours into the night, people passing by and staying to chat, some sticking for awhile, some just saying hello. I saw several people I knew, some I hadn't seen for a while. I only had one other beer, then switched to coffee, my main food.

About ten-thirty, Hal, Walter, and a lady shooter named Emily were discussing Canadian shoots. We were arranged around the fire, the Coleman lanterns turned off for the night, everyone relaxed.

"You know," Hal said, "I remember the first time I went to Canada. My wife and I were going to a shoot in Ontario, and I was confused from the moment I crossed the border.

"They were pleasant enough people, but everything was just slightly off. The roads didn't go east, west, north, and south like you'd expect, but went off at kitty-cornered angles.

"When they gave the temperature on the radio it was in Celsius, and neither of us could remember exactly how to convert. And the money—whew! They might call them dollars, but when we stopped for gas I didn't know what I was getting back for change, or whether it was the right amount—and it didn't help that the gas was measured in liters instead of gallons, either."

"I heard they did an experiment," Emily interjected. "They started in England with a hundred pounds, then went to France, Germany, Belgium, and back to England. All they did was exchange the money in each country—they didn't buy anything with it. When they changed the money back into pounds at the end of the trip, there was only about half of it left."

"Yeah," Hal said. "That's what it felt like—I didn't know what was going on. When we got on the big road, the QEW, I thought we had gotten in the middle of a funeral somehow."

Walter laughed. "The daytime running lights?"

"Yeah," Hal said. "Boy, I was confused. Anyway, I had all this going through my head—how the laws might be different, the temperature change, the lights on the cars, the money, the gas, and then I saw an exit sign for a city. On the bottom of it it said 'Population 150,000.' I know it sounds silly, but my first thought was to try to figure out how many real people that was!"

I almost choked on my coffee then.

After a few minutes Walter spoke. "You know, it's a funny thing about money. It seems like it grows, y'know?"

"Not mine," Hal said.

"I mean the change, dufus. You know—you start off with just a little change in your pocket, and then you buy something with bills instead of using coins, which adds to the ones you already have, and then—poof—all of a sudden your pockets are just full of change?"

"Okay—so what?"

"Well—I've got a theory. Suppose some of them are male, and some are female."

"O-kay..." Hal was waiting for this one—it sounded like his best friend had come up with a real doozy.

"Okay, except that only some of them are fertile, you know? Maybe it's like only a queen bee can have kids."

"O-kay..."

"Okay. So maybe it's like a critical mass thing or something, but when you get a certain number of coins in your pocket, all of a sudden they start multiplying, and you've got tons of 'em in your pocket."

"And then?"

"Well, then you start spending it, and it seems like you just have handful after handful, and then, at some point, it all starts disappearing, like they not only stopped multiplying, but evaporated!"

"Sounds like a tough theory to prove."

"So what—just think about it... You go along, spending all that money, then at some point you spend the queen bee, you know? After that they can't multiply anymore, and they get spent!"

We laughed. "'You just keep thinkin', Butch, that's what you're good at,'" Hal said, using the old line from *Butch Cassidy and the Sundance Kid*.

We chatted for a while longer. At some point Hal went into the RV for the night, and I could feel the evening was about to end. It felt so wonderful to sit at this fire, to see these folks again.

I said my goodnights and went back to my own RV, ready for a good night's sleep.

I had an idea while I was walking, and wrote it in my notebook when I got back to my camp. It was to do a series of 'environmental portraits'—not photographs of people, but portraits of their "stuff," the everyday items they used.

I immediately thought of my Dad, and what I would use for his portrait. My father had died less than a year ago, and the pain was still fresh—his memory was still very much with me.

Dad had been a real character. He had always had his own business, started in his early twenties, probably one of the reasons I had never felt comfortable with the idea of working for someone else.

He repaired and installed water pumps, a good business in Florida where a lot of people had their own wells. The depression affected him deeply, like a lot of his contemporaries, and he had earned a reputation as someone who could repair a pump when no one else could. When he died, I knew a lot of his old customers would finally have to replace their ancient systems, finally have to abandon the old equipment that only he could keep alive. He had been respected and loved for many reasons by many people.

I had sometimes worked with him while I was growing up. I remembered how he would use a self-modified Chrysler New Yorker as his work truck, the first one I remembered from 1964. When he bought a new one, he prepared it by removing the back seat, covering the interior with thick-gauge clear plastic, adding heavy-duty truck springs to the suspension, and mounting extra-large ambulance rims and tires.

His work uniform included jodhpurs, English riding boots, and long-sleeved shirts buttoned to the top, sometimes even with a tie, an unusual outfit for the tropics. Mom didn't see the comparison, but I think whatever idiosyncrasies of dress I had were just a reflection of what I learned from being with him. I loved him, and would always miss him.

I started a list in my notebook—I was tired, but I knew I would have to pay attention to this idea before I could rest.

I wanted a photograph that would be recognizable to anyone who knew him well. I wanted someone to see that photograph and know immediately who it represented with no hesitation.

The initial list included the riding boots, the half-glasses he would push up his nose when he wanted to see details, one of the white handkerchiefs he always had available, a worn and battered red eighteen-inch crescent wrench, and maybe one of the old-fashioned pitcher pumps he would use to pull water through an electric or gas-powered pump, to help it prime.

I envisioned the still life, mentally rearranging the elements and the environment where I would shoot them, composing and recomposing. I made a sketch to add to the idea then set it next to the bed. It would be entirely possible I would awaken with an idea sometime during the night, and the notebook needed to always be there.

*I remembered something that happened long ago, when I helped Dad in the summers and before I trained in other things. Sitting cross-legged and bent over in the shallow area, I placed the five-foot bar between the top of the pump and the roof of the eighteen-inch crawl space where it had been installed many years before. The bar weighed about forty pounds and had originally been used to pry up large spikes, back when my grandfather had worked on the railroad. I had been able to remove the pieces of two-by-four on which the pump had rested, but everything was still tightly-packed, the pump held up to the low roof by tightly-frozen pipe fittings.*

*Pushing down on the bar with my left hand, I could use it as a lever to move the pump down enough for me to reach the fitting on the top of the pump with the large crescent wrench. I set the wrench in place with my right hand, the opening of its jaws facing away from me, and made sure it was solidly set on the frozen fitting. I released the bar, allowing the pump to raise back up. The two tools formed a shallow 'V' shape, and I was between them.*

*I studied the fitting, then slid a "come-along," as Dad called it, on the end of the wrench, a four-foot length of two-inch pipe we used to give us a mechanical advantage. I placed my elbow over the top of the solid bar, leaning down until the pump moved, then pushed away from my body on the end of the come-along, making sure to apply even pressure.*

*There was danger in this arrangement if I pushed too hard sideways on the big bar, so I had to be careful—I didn't want it to slip out. I built up pressure—downward on the big bar, sideways away from me on the two-inch pipe—until it became obvious the fitting wasn't going to budge.*

*I reached up with my right hand, underhanded, and grabbed one of the two-by-four floor supports above my head, pulling the unyielding support towards me so I wouldn't shift backwards, then braced my right foot against the come-along. I concentrated, making sure everything was properly set, and then pushed down on the bar, and over with my bare foot.*

*The pressure built up and the fitting broke free, releasing the pent-up energy.*

When I awakened the next morning, I looked over my sketch and notes. I brushed my teeth, took a shower, and then added a couple of things to the notes while I made coffee, new things that had occurred to me, things that reminded me of my dad.

When I parked at the far end of the field, I pulled around so my door, awning, and camp faced towards the woods, away from the field. I wasn't trying to be antisocial, but liked to plan things so I could have some privacy in case things got a little crazy. As it was turning out, I felt I needed some of that privacy now, this morning.

Thinking about my father had reminded me how deeply I was still feeling his loss. I didn't really want to be with anyone else right now, even my archer friends. It would have been different if Melissa was with me, but she was far away. I'd have to deal with this on my own, without her welcome distractions.

The RV was set up so the inside dining area faced away from the main door, so as I drank my coffee I looked through the window out over the few campers that had set up in the dew-covered field. I expected many more by the end of the day.

After I rinsed my cup I went outside and sat in one of the folding chairs, looking into the woods, staring at nothing for a little while.

I eventually noticed a curve just inside the tree line that marked the base of a low hill heading up towards the road, and that reminded me of that little barn I had photographed yesterday afternoon. I bet myself a nickel I could find that barn again by going through the woods. A little orienteering challenge like that would get my mind off of things, perhaps, and make me fit company again.

I thought about the position of the barn and mentally mapped out the road to Denton Hill I took after leaving it, along with the twists and turns I followed after entering the grounds. If I figured correctly, it shouldn't be more than a mile or so away. This could be fun—and if not fun, at least distracting. I went inside the RV to get ready.

I had spent a lot of time in the woods over the years and felt comfortable there. I always went prepared, but minimally so, making the smallest pack I felt I could get away with.

When I was anywhere near the woods, including, of course, a weekend like this, I wore three things on my belt; a sheath knife, a black multi-function pocket knife in its case, and a small five-inch by eight-inch cordura nylon belt pack. The sheath knife I wore today was a skinner with a deep-bellied four-inch blade—simple and sharp—big enough to do the job, small enough to stay out of my way. The pocket knife was the largest available with all the bells and whistles, and the case had other supplies, like a sharpener, compass, ruler, band-aids, needle, thread, and some other small items. The small belt pack had a small camera, an emergency survival blanket that folded into its own tiny package, a thin little tea-towel, a signal mirror, a collapsible cup, some water purification tablets, fifty feet of thin cord, two tiny butane lighters, a fold-up toothbrush and toothpaste, a small long-burning candle, a tiny flashlight with two spare batteries, a miniature deck of cards, some antibiotic cream, and a little package of fire-starter material.

I felt I could stay out at least overnight with this kit, if I needed to, and since this little trek would only last a few hours at most, I thought I would be okay. If I were actually packing to go out overnight, then I would take more, but I hated carrying too much.

I looked around, seeing what else I wanted to take. The only other things I could come up with were a pair of flip-flops, in case the ground got prickly, the miniature thirty-five millimeter camera, a spare roll of film, and a small roll-up hammock that collapsed to about the size of a baseball—just in case I wanted to take a nap. I loved naps, but didn't want to wear a day pack just to carry the little hammock, so I decided to wear a black tank top and my black BDUs—military-style pants with pockets everywhere. That way I could put the flip-flops and camera in one knee-pocket, and the hammock in the other, along, perhaps, with some extra pipe tobacco. Maybe I would take a paperback, too.

I could have taken the cellular phone, but had already tested it and found there wasn't a signal here, so it would be useless. I didn't worry about food, and never did unless I was staying out longer than overnight—even then I might just take some cheese or something. I didn't seem to get very hungry or thirsty in the woods, nor did I seem to have to eliminate my bodily wastes very often.

Okay, now—which bow should I take?

Considering what I was doing, I decided to take the little Kiko Tovar 44 Magnum. It was the cutest little thing, only about forty-one inches strung, lightweight and handy, but with a healthy sixty-three pound draw weight. It had a modernistic shape with a riser made from black phenolic and fast little limbs made from multiple maple laminations, also black. There was a black bow quiver attached that carried seven arrows. It looked like I was going to be all-black today—not the best color to hide in the woods, but I wasn't hunting today, just strolling.

I strung the bow. A special short stringer came with the bow, but worked like most others. I slipped the small leather cup on each end of a cord onto the tips of the limbs. With my foot on the floor and resting on the stringer cord, I pulled the bow up, flexing the limbs and allowing me to push the top loop of the bowstring up onto the grooved tip. When I was sure the loops of the string were positioned properly, I released the tension on the cord by lowering the bow. I tested the draw—it was ready.

Kiko was a master hunter and bowyer with an international reputation, and I was lucky to have a bow that he made especially for me. He was a respecter of things Native American, and a man who knew the holiness of nature. This bow was made for brush hunting, and I was going into the brush, so it was perfect.

The arrows I had made for this bow had a base stain of deep walnut color accented with large sections of black and thin stripes of white and gold. They were fletched with dark natural-barred turkey feathers cut to a five-inch shield shape. I selected three broadhead-tipped shafts, two target shafts, and two yado shafts with narrow slicing tips on one end and two-inch long cylindrical steel tips at the other. The front points on all the arrows fit up into a hood at the top of the quiver, out of sight and protected.

Ready now, I went outside and took a few practice shots into a foam-filled practice target. Each bow shot just a little differently, and it always took a few shots to warm up. The act of taking some warm-up shots was calming, anyway, even if it wasn't something I needed to do.

Feeling better already, I left my camp, silently crossed the tree line and entered the woods.

I could have kept track of where I was going with a topographical map and compass, but didn't want to be that formal. I knew where the road was, approximately, and knew I was heading in a direction opposite to where the other shooters were. If I got lost it would just be an adventure, but I hadn't gotten lost for years. I always seemed to know directions, and if something looked unfamiliar on the return route, I would just sit down, smoke a bowl of tobacco, and think about it for a few minutes, sure to eventually find my way.

I went to a spot near the top of this first hill, then squatted to see what I could see under the trees. There was another hill in the direction I thought I should take, so I climbed it, taking care to notice sounds, smells, or any evidence of an animal's passing.

At the top of the fourth hill I entered a flat area, stopped and listened. I heard the sound of a truck passing in the distance, slightly to my right, but I couldn't tell just how far away it was. I went in that direction, listening and walking between the trees.

After about two hundred yards I saw the barn in front of me and to my left—bingo! I had found it just about where I thought it would be. I checked my watch, then turned around, mentally going back over my route and thinking how it could be shortened. When I thought I had my return route picked out I went over to the barn and took a few new pictures, then sat on the ground and had a smoke.

Finished, I walked back over the flat area, stopping just before it dropped off to curve downhill, then strung the hammock for some light reading and a nap. It was 11:00 now, and I didn't really need to be back at the shoot until late this afternoon. I admitted to myself that I felt better now, over my funk and more than a little pleased with myself.

The hammock was comfortable except that it was difficult to keep it flat enough—it tended to roll up around me. I finally got out and found a couple of fairly straight sticks of the right diameter, then interlaced them through the holes near either ends of the hammock. This worked wonderfully well to help flatten it, and I fell asleep after reading for about fifteen minutes.

After I took my nap I rubbed a little toothpaste on my teeth—when I reached some clean water I'd brush them for real. I stretched thoroughly, then packed the hammock. I checked the area, smoothing out any trace that I had been here—I never liked to make noise or to leave a track, when I had the chance. Finished, I re-oriented myself and started down the hill in a slightly new direction. I thought I could save myself a little distance, if not time, by taking this shortcut—another adventure.

I carried the bow in my left hand, but wasn't wearing my shooting glove. I used nocking markers made of dental floss wound around the string—pretty gentle on my fingers. I knew I could take several shots without getting sore.

I felt wonderful.

I was able this time to stay away from the tops of the hills, just taking a pleasant stroll. About halfway back, though, I heard a noise just over the next little rise, and I stopped, very still, casting about for any ki I could feel. I listened for a few more minutes, careful not to make any noise, then heard leaves being kicked up, first way up to my right, then again out of sight on the left, small fast-moving shadows flitting across my mind.

I quietly slid a broadhead-tipped shaft out of the bow quiver and nocked it on the string, then moved forward silently, extending my senses to the front, then all around.

Inching up the incline, I checked again in all directions, then looked over the rise, ready to shoot.

I saw and smelled a small carcass—a fawn or a small doe, by the looks of it. Torn almost apart, there was blood everywhere. There was so much gore I couldn't believe just one animal had done this, and I immediately thought—dogs.

Dogs have always been a part of my life, sometimes an important part, and I feel I know them well. As individuals they are wonderful beings that can be caring and protective of their families. It's easy to believe they are always our friends, dependents, and protectors, but that's not the case.

I've always thought of dogs as being similar to little boys. When there is only one, everything is fine except for an occasional accident. Two together could possibly mean trouble, like a tug-of-war or a broken vase—nothing intentionally malicious. Three or more, however, virtually guarantees mischief and the only thing worse than three or more would be three or more away from home, away from any civilized supervision—then the innocent mischief can turn into deliberate viciousness.

I knew there were two possibilities if these were dogs. The first, whether they were errant pets or feral predators, was that the dogs had found the carcass and torn it up without malice, just eating and establishing their social status with each other. If this was what was happening, then it's possible I had chased them off, probably with my scent, and their running away would have been the sound I heard in the distance.

I hoped this was the case, because the alternative was that these dogs had turned into a hunting pack. If so, then they wouldn't be very pleased I was invading their kill.

I was worried about the possibilities, because when dogs were innocently involved in an activity they tended to be oblivious to everything else These had moved quietly away without being chased, though, and were perhaps even attempting to scout me.

I was alone here, probably a half-mile from anyone who could help, so whatever happened was in my hands. I slowly turned around to make sure I couldn't see any of them, then moved back down the way I had come. I wanted to make it as clear as possible I had no interest in the meat they had left. If it meant going back up to the old barn and walking down the main road, then I would gladly walk the long way, the entire distance around to the front gate at Denton Hill.

I followed the path I had just taken exactly in reverse, knowing my scent would already be there. I didn't walk any more quickly or slowly than I had just a few minutes before, trying to emanate a sense of innocence. The only difference in my outward appearance now would be that the bow was ready to shoot, sharpened tip pointed safely towards the ground.

As I entered the next hollow I felt and saw two dogs—one under the edge of a bush thirty yards away to the right and forward, one halfway up the hill to my left. I wasn't immediately worried about the dog up the hill, a long-haired little all-brown shepherd mix, because he had positioned himself just over the side of the hill and was standing there tongue out, looking a little like he wanted to play.

The other one, though, was larger, a black and tan shorthair with a long snout—perhaps a Doberman, but not purebred. He had his head raised just a few inches off the ground, staring at me.

I was careful to watch them with just my peripheral vision and not to give them a challenging stare as I walked a few more steps, veering a little to the left to pass the larger dog at a better distance. I didn't really want to walk between them, but couldn't turn my back, either. As I started to pass the first dog, the more playful one took off, perhaps flustered I was coming closer to him.

Suddenly two more dogs appeared at the top of the hill, directly in my path. They stood there, still. I didn't look at them but stopped and squatted quickly, then held out my right hand to the closest dog, the large one under the bush.

"Here, boy, c'mon..."

He raised up slightly, like he was going to stand up, maybe even let me play with him, but then sank back into a crouch, ready to spring. It hadn't worked. I guess there wasn't much of the house pet left in him, if it indeed had ever been there. These woods covered a lot of ground, and a pack like this could go undetected for a long, long time if they were careful. My misfortune was probably showing up alone and in the middle of their kill. I readied myself.

He sprang at me. I saw the two dogs at the top of the hill start running in my direction at the same time. First things first.

*The arrow caught the first dog in mid-air as he was hurtling towards my throat, just feet away from me. I dropped to the ground as he flew over me and pulled another hunting shaft from the quiver, mounted it and shot all in one motion, shot from the ground, impaling the closer of the two dogs running at me full speed, entering his eye socket, flipping him away from me, stopping him immediately.*

*Nocking the third broadhead as I rolled back upright, I faced the second dog that had run at me. He was obviously reconsidering since his friends were stopped, momentarily flustered.*

*His friend was dead, there was no doubt, but the first dog was trying to thrash about and bite the end of the arrow sticking out of his chest. He was dead, too, but didn't realize it yet.*

*This dog was way too close. I took the opportunity to set the bow and nocked arrow down slowly while I pulled the two yado shafts from the quiver. I shifted them and stood, poised and ready with feet in the proper kata position, one in each hand grasped near the back of the shaft, sharp-bladed points held away from my body at forty-five degree angles.*

*The little shepherd-mix dog returned from over the hill at a full run, probably thinking the bow had been the weapon to fear, now out of my reach on the ground. From his demeanor I had thought he ran away, but he was back, looking for an easy kill. He stopped next to the other dog, then circled a little to his left, my right, trying to find an unprotected side—I had obviously and seriously underestimated what I had thought to be his friendly nature. I backed away carefully, circumventing the dog still thrashing about weakly. I didn't want to risk tripping over the bow or a freshly-dead body.*

*Both dogs lunged at me, not wanting me to get too far away. The little dog jumped sideways with a sliced neck, confused by all the blood squirting from a wound he probably felt as just a slight tug. The last dog slumped to the ground, the tendons of his front legs cut, then jerked sideways as the yado blade entered his ear through to his brain.*

*It only took a few moments for all four dogs to be still, all life gone. I stood still until my heart wasn't pounding in my throat anymore, listening and feeling for any more that might still be out there somewhere.*

Satisfied I was alone, though still wary, I pulled out the tiny sliver of tea-towel and cleaned the yado shafts, paying special attention to the steel blades—nothing corroded steel faster than blood, something I had learned from years of hunting. The steel used in the yado blades was so polished that the sticky liquid seemed to run right off, though. I supposed I could be forgiven for not knowing this, since they had never had blood on them—not since I had owned them, anyway.

I made very sure all the dogs were dead before I pulled the two arrows from the remaining bodies. Knowing they were dead was one thing, but when you had to touch them you had better be sure. The dog with the eye injury was particularly tough, because the Sniper two-bladed broadhead wanted to stick inside his skull, and it took some wiggling to get it out.

I cleaned the arrows as best I could, but was frustrated by the sticky blood on the black-coated broadheads. They were finished with teflon, I thought, but it was still difficult to get them perfectly clean. I'd finish the cleaning job when I got back to the RV, but mentally added a small bottle of water or some wet-wipes to my belt pack for the future.

I had killed before, hunting, but always with prayers and what I thought was the proper attitude. This is the first time I had ever had to use my skills in self-defense, and I kneeled where I could see the bodies, trying to figure out what I should feel.

These dogs had tried to kill me, to make me their food, but I had killed them instead.

I had been to them what a buck was to me during hunting season, probably nothing more. Their tools and hunting methods were different, but our goals were the same. I wondered if they had understood the "thumb up-thumbs down" nature of their hunting, whether they had ever conceived of losing?

Like most people, violence was not normally something that was part of my life, so my feelings were very mixed. My training had allowed me to defeat four adversaries, hunters who were probably very good at what they did, and in that sense I was pleased. What I didn't understand was why I was the one that deserved to live. Was my life more important than the buck's life that I took—more important than even the lives of these dogs?

My most pessimistic view of life was Man-As-Virus. In it I saw man as an infector of the Earth, much like a tiny virus infects a much larger living host. As the host wastes away because of infection, the virus is driven to migrate to a new host, to spread, to infect anew. I would have been embarrassed to admit it out loud, but as much as the technology of the space program intrigued me, when I saw the lift-off of a shuttle, a new rocket, or perhaps the launching of a deep-space probe, the thought of our species trying to spread beyond our infected host was obvious to me.

I meditated for a while, kneeling there, studying the remains of my adversaries, three of the four pathetically small in death, the fourth one huge. Too shaken to clean the area as I normally would, I checked myself over to make sure I looked somewhat normal, no extra dirt smudge or mark of Cain, then walked back towards the RV that I had left a lifetime ago.

The walk was pleasant, even exhilarating, and I finally decided that it was me saying "Yes!" to life, to the fact I was alive. I was fully here, and in some way I deserved my place. I could enjoy this beauty. I was alive now, but might not have been, so in some very basic way I had earned the right to be this happy now.

My most optimistic view of life was a Holy one. Most of the time I felt we were here to connect with everything else, to caretake and to nurture, one of the reasons I thought it was so easy for me to feel other beings without having to see them. I learned many things from Christ and his parables, and tried to pay attention to the other things that spoke to me, no matter what their origin, looking at them as parables, always searching for new lessons or reaffirmations of old ones. I wanted to walk in Awareness, really connecting with it All, really Understanding. There was no place that Church didn't exist for me.

When I returned I re-cleaned everything and made sure my little pack was in order, then unstrung the little bow, thanking it. I would practice with Sensei GreyBeard for the rest of the day, I thought, and got it ready.

I washed, changed clothes, then fixed a rather late lunch, a sautéed salmon fillet (adding just a wee bit of butter and salt), eaten from my special bowl to help me re-center myself. I had a set of eating utensils made by a friend who worked in wood, and I used them at every private or family meal to remind me of the simplicity of a proper life. There was a ten-inch wide plate, a seven-inch bowl, and a three-inch cup, all turned out of cherry—simple, elegant, well-made, and Holy to me. He had also made a set of Ebony o-hashi—chopsticks. I ate in silence, savoring the taste and the firmness of the salmon.

I was aware of the mega-life I have, of the abundance I enjoy, though sometimes embarrassed by the wealth of it. I wouldn't change any of my world, but felt the need to use things like these utensils to help me keep sight of the spiritual core of life.

After cleaning the bowl, I wandered back over to the shoot. I saw some of those I had already seen, and greeted some new arrivals. The sense of normalcy amazed me after the adventure I had had just a few hours ago—it seemed as though the world had changed to me, and no one had even noticed I had been gone! There was no reason they should have, I guess, but it still amazed me.

I wasn't going to tell anyone about the dogs, of course, because there might be some way the art I was obligated to keep secret would be discovered. I took this obligation very seriously, and figured there wouldn't be anything to be gained from telling the folks here about my day. All I wanted to do was regain some sort of equilibrium—quite a day.

I shot for awhile, then wandered again, this time to the vendors tents that were filling up quickly. There were two main tents at the base of the hill between the main parking area and the practice range on my side of the lodge, with three or four smaller tents at their far end. I was supposed to meet someone here, a bowmaker friend from Canada.

While reading a traditional bowhunting magazine I had come across a small ad for a company that seemed to have a Japanese connection. The ad didn't say very much, but had a very sumi-e-like logo that intrigued me. Of course I had to find out what the deal was, why a company based so far north would have a connection to my belovéd kyudo. When I called, I telephonically met the bowmaker and his wife, and after we had talked for hours had arranged to meet here.

They turned out to be thoroughly enjoyable people. He was originally from Holland, and had come to this country to run a greenhouse, eventually becoming fascinated by archery. His wife was an assistant professor of religion and culture at a university near their home and she loved things relating to India as well as archery. Their dog, a silver-tipped husky, was thoroughly spoiled and loved.

I was surprised, but meeting their dog didn't bother me in the least—in fact I took extra pleasure in rubbing her thick coat, being able to play with her and not worry about her intentions. She was a joy, oblivious to any unusual smells I might have gathered during my adventures.

We talked long into the extended daylight of summer, setting up their tent, dealing with an evening meal, talking about archery.

He and and his wife weren't going to shoot the course this weekend, but were going to be selling bows and taking orders at their booth, so there would be plenty of time to talk, and we tried to spend our time well.

Between them they knew so much about archery, their knowledge not limited to the little bit I knew as "traditional archery." There was the yumi, of course, but there were also composite bows from a wide range of lands from China over to the Middle East; recurves patterned after those the Egyptians used, longbows, bushbows, selfbows, even a class of short recurve patterned after a Mongolian bow. Some bows were available for sale here, and others could be ordered, but with patience—there was as much as a three-year wait for the sinew-layered traditional composite bows.

The bow I fell in love with was the south Indian bow, a classic double-curve bow with outer laminations of bamboo, a design used at least as early as 1200A.D. in southern India, a tall seventy-inch design that gradually spread up through central Asia. The internal laminations were more modern material, but the bow had such an amazing feel to it that I was immediately taken.

It did not have a "shelf" cut into it, the little ledge that modern traditional bows used to rest the arrow, but I was used to shooting "off the hand" from Japanese archery. I was surprised when I found out from my new friends that the shelf wasn't invented until the mid-1920's, discovering that before this time there were no bows that used it. When I saw these bows I immediately knew this was traditional archery as most of the historical world knew it, the real stuff. The double-curve design was just so classic and pure, what a bow was meant to be, that I could imagine this bow being carried on the back of an elephant into war. It certainly must have come from a tradition similar to my Yumi, a tradition that respected the Way of the Bow. I bought this Indian bow and ordered a similar bow with a lighter draw weight for my Melissa.

They knew so much about historical archery that I was flabbergasted. This bowmaker was intensely concerned with why a bow was designed as it was, and what secrets a traditional bowmaker knew that might have been lost to time. He was anxious to discover any and all possible secrets, to take archers back to the time when a shot could be taken accurately out to sometimes several hundreds of yards. He and his wife did extensive research on all things archery, and she would publish articles from time to time in archery-related publications.

They even knew which bows had been used with thumb-rings, those mysterious little pieces of jewelry some oriental archers used to release the string. I had seen one once in a book published in the mid-sixties, but had not seen the real thing until I visited the Fred Bear archery museum in Gainesville, Florida this past year, a few rings in a glass case with little information.

Here I was talking to a guy that could make those rings, and even knew how they were used in different cultures. I was ecstatic, a sponge.

This was not "primitive archery," the way the term was used today. I had been to several buckskinner-type gatherings, and many of the folks there seemed to equate primitive with poorly-made. I knew that anything as important as archery would have had a great deal of attention paid to it, and that the word primitive was a misnomer at best. Here were people who were anxious to tell the world about our heritage—to unite us, in a way.

They both responded well to my arrows, and we discussed several projects that would lend themselves to collaboration, discussed them over the long weekend.

*Archers are always trying to come up with modifications to improve their equipment, especially in Europe and America. This is pretty natural,*

*I suppose, because we have to do a certain amount of modification on almost a daily basis—the size, shape, or construction of the fletching on the arrow, the weight of the arrow tip, the material or shape of the grip, or even slight variations in the shooting glove.*

*Compound shooters are especially prone to this, of course, because their mechanical equipment needs to be tuned and cajoled—there are cables, cams, bearings, rests, releases, sights, stabilizers, and other things that beg to be tweaked, replaced, or updated.*

*When I was in high school I very cautiously sent a letter to Ben Pearson, an archery company with a fine reputation. I had developments I wanted to sell—would they be interested in buying?*

*They sent back an agreement I could sign so my patent rights would be protected, and I sent it back to them with drawings outlining my three inventions. Pretty nice of them, I thought.*

*The first idea was to combine a bow with a circular hole in the middle, replacing the arrow rest, and an arrow with a small metal collar near the tip. The hole would be surrounded by magnets, so when the arrow was drawn back and the collar hit the magnets it would ping up into position, held stationary by the magnetic field in the hole.*

*The second idea was an arrow with a connector in the middle to allow the arrow to be taken down into two pieces. A twist of the wrist and it would be apart; align the halves, twist, and there's a whole arrow again.*

*The third innovation was to apply fletch to an arrow in a spiral to impart spin when it flew through the air.*

*When they answered my letter, I must say they were very gracious, much more than many would be to a seventeen-year old.*

*The complex hole-in-the-bow idea? Not possible because of archer's paradox making the arrow bend on release.*

*The breakdown arrow? Already in existence.*

*And my masterpiece, the spiral fletch? That was an idea so old that the corpse named The Iceman recently found frozen on the Austrian-Italian border had them with him. Some estimates put him at twelve thousand years old.*

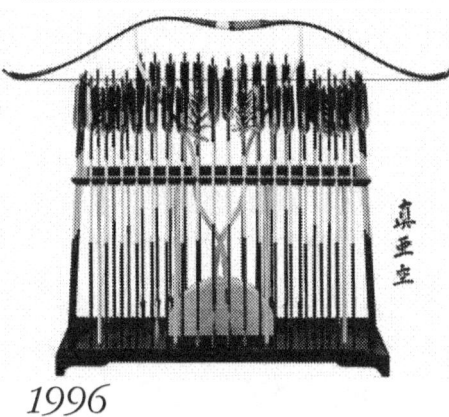

真亜空

*1996*

# Kentucky-Florida

*In many Native American mythologies, the concept of the Medicine Wheel is central. There are big wheels and small wheels, wheels that represent a world or a nation or a community or a family or an individual—wheels within wheels, wheels connected to wheels.*

*We are taught that we are born at a particular place on our own wheel of life, and that gives us the powers natural to us, the gifts that we carry on our journey. From our starting point it is our responsibility to move around the wheel, to learn the lessons of the other powers, to add to our gifts, all the while remaining at the center of the universe.*

*Part of the teaching of the Medicine Wheel concerns perception. If we were all to gather around the circle and look at something in its center we would all have different perceptions, we would all see the object from our own unique angle. Some of our references would be similar because of our shared cultures or knowledge, but some others would be unique to me, some unique to you, depending on an accumulation of experiences and our own personal "point of view."*

*Sometimes it's tough to make that next move on the wheel.*

*I* replaced the strung Millennium bow on its rack along with the target shafts I had been using. The Millennium was a collaboration between four of us, and was a wonderful culmination of a lot of cooperation, research, work, and time.

The bow itself was the historically classic double-curve shape like the first bow I had gotten from my Canadian bowmaker friend, although it was smaller and slightly asymmetrical so the arrow rested just below the center of the bow. This bow was only fifty-five inches when strung, slender, rounded, and elegant, a blend of design and construction elements from around the world.

This was one of the areas in which my friends excelled. Between them they had academic and practical research skills blended with intimate knowledge of the mechanical and artistic requirements of a bow, ancient or modern. This allowed him to craft a bow combining complementary elements that may have never been combined anywhere in history.

The belly (or face) of the bow, the part facing the archer when the bow is drawn, was made of the gently-shaped horn of a water buffalo, as were the Asiatic style curved tips. The bow's back, the side facing away from the archer, was made from the same type of bamboo used in a Japanese yumi. The sandwiched part between the faces was also of Japanese construction, with African Ebony outer edges and a layered bamboo inner core. The shelf-less grip was wrapped with rough rayskin to provide a stable grip, and there was a small inlaid ivory escutcheon plate set in the lower limb for scrimshaw.

The overall effect of this bow was that of a something plucked right off the historical image of an Asian horse archer, riding at full gallop across the steppes and deserts of Asia. It was an elegant thing, bound at strategic points with rattan strips and black silk thread, the laminations glued with natural glues.

The stand itself was made by a furniture designer and woodworker from the Boston area, the same friend who had made my eating utensils. The hardwood base of the stand was a rectangle with shaped feet, eleven inches deep, three inches high, and forty inches wide, with dimples to hold the tips of the arrows that were part of the set. From the center of the stand rose an unstained maple centerpiece, two limbs curving up like the antlers of a gazelle out of a semicircular base, with notches hollowed out of their thirty-seven inch-high tips to cradle the bow horizontally, strung or unstrung. Around the perimeter of the stand and nineteen inches above the base was a rectangular structure, stained to match the base, supported by natural-finish light hardwood dowels, and notched to hold the upper portions of the arrows. The entire stand was oil-finished and a worthy piece of furniture in its own right.

The original concept of The Millennium set was mine, but the arrows were my physical contribution to the set. There were forty-two of them—twenty-four target, twelve hunting, and six flu-flu shafts. Flu-flus are arrows fletched with over-large feathers on the back to slow the arrows down as they are shot at aerial targets, to keep them from traveling long distances, possibly endangering unintended targets and easy to retrieve. The shafts all matched, selectively stained to match the bow and stand, crested in black and gold.

The sales of my arrows had become so successful that I had no way of keeping up with the demand and had hired two people full-time to craft them for me. The designs were mine, of course, but archers and non-archers alike seemed to appreciate their unique qualities, so I had no choice but to expand the number of hands available to make them. They were sold individually or in sets, with various stands and shadowboxes available to display them.

I made the arrows for The Millennium myself, carefully crafting each one out of close-grained Port Orford cedar shafts originally turned over sixty years ago by a master shaftmaker—fine shafts unavailable today, matched for physical weight, spine weight, and diameter. Matching each to the others, the bow and the stand was something I thoroughly enjoyed.

Twelve of the arrows were tipped with matching broadheads, almost three inches long and three-quarters of an inch wide, handmade and razor sharp. The tanged blades were leaf-shaped like the top of a fleur-de-lis and flared slightly at the bottom. Two of the flu-flu shafts were tipped with "bird points," smaller diamond-shaped blades designed for shooting small game.

All these points were made by the fourth member of the team, a knifemaker from Quebec. His work was exquisite, and his talents showed in each of these tips.

Altogether, the effect of the ensemble was complete. It was a combination of parts that were each unique, worthy of a warrior—an heirloom to last through the generations.

The bow was smooth, quiet, and quick, as well as beautiful, and it was a joy to shoot—my friend had done well with it. He and his wife had become friends—Melissa and I would visit them, they would visit us. Theirs was one of the most committed relationships I had ever seen, a partnership of over twenty years, one of those marriages you just knew would be life-long.

They had introduced Melissa and I to many craftsfolk, including flint-knappers and obsidian workers, leather workers and carvers, bowyers, arrowmakers, material and craft suppliers of all descriptions—even an Eastern Orthodox icon painter. There was an incredible network of artisans growing, a world-wide set of capable people who cared about preserving traditional knowledge and skills. It felt like an updated version of the sixties, dealing as we were with caring people who were concerned about their relationships and practicing their crafts in an extended community—extended all over the world, for some of us.

Interest in historical and traditional archery itself had grown rapidly, and the heightened demand had brought some less-than-scrupulous makers into the market, so a group of us had formed the Archery Guild, an organization of like-minded people who wanted to protect the reputations of reputable dealers and makers. It had originally started with just a few people, but had rapidly grown to a national, even international, organization, and we were to have a groundbreaking for our own museum in Florida this winter.

The most influential archer anyone had known was Kiko, the maker of the little Dog Bow, as I now called it. It was originally thought he might accept a leadership rôle in the organization, but, sadly, he had died in February of last year, a tragic event for all those who loved him, as well as those who knew him from his ever-growing reputation.

We had been at our bowmaker friend's mid-Ontario house for a Native American pipe ceremony one weekend, a ceremony originally intended solely to give thanks for his wife's recovery from a potentially life-threatening disease she had contracted on a Christmas-time visit to India. She had been invited to a conference, and her fifteen-day trip had almost turned deadly—as it was, things had been touch-and-go for a while. Missy and I were honored they had invited us to the ceremony.

The news of Kiko's death at that time gave all of us an increased sense of the dramatic nature of things and the seriousness of our purpose—it solemnified the nature of our thanks, while adding prayers for our lost friend.

I had designed the logo for the Guild, twelve inward-pointing arrowheads arranged in an circle, all tied together with a red circle.

A secondary mission of the Guild was the gathering and publishing of information, and I was putting the finishing touches on an interactive multimedia CD-ROM for the organization. It included several reference works, including out-of-copyright books about archery as well as video and audio clips of some famous archers, some very instructional. Many of these references had not been available to the public before, and we wanted to get as much information to as many people as possible. This was only the beginning of a very long-term project, but it was a good start and merged my twin interests of archery and computers.

We had four major concurrent projects running. Two of these, the building of the museum and the gathering of material for exhibits, had the highest priority. I had been able to get on the committee to handle the design of the structure and grounds, located somewhat near the Fred Bear museum, and was pleased with our progress—the architectural renderings would be available at the groundbreaking, an exciting time for all of us. The third project was one of historical research, and there was a special push to get information from some countries, especially South Korea, India, and China, because their governments officially felt archery was an antiquated art, and any practice or publicity about that art could only made them look less-than-modern. The dissemination of information was the last project, and the CD-ROM and the internet would be a big part of that, although the museum would sell many books, tapes, and other items.

There was a wealth of information that would eventually be on the disc, but much of it was still being collated and gathered. This first CD-ROM would include many things, but would only be the first step, with much more planned for the future.

We were trying not to be concerned about the large amounts of data we were gathering, because even though we were quickly running out of room on our first CD-ROM, we knew that the DVD, the Digital Versatile Disc, was just around the corner. The CD held about 650 megabytes of information, quite a lot, but the double-sided double density DVD would (they said) hold as much as four-and-a-half gigabytes of information, or about seven times as much as a CD.

I had really gotten into computers, and was always excited about one project or another. The future seemed bright for technology and its ability to not only store knowledge in new ways but to make both old and new information available to a larger percentage of the world than was ever historically possible.

We had expanded the house a few years before, after we had our fourth child. There were now more bedrooms and another bath upstairs, which left room for an amazing den-office downstairs. We both had computers of our own there, and everything was connected by a high-speed network to the computers in the office on the other side of the house. There were eight employees in that office now, handling orders from the catalogue and the website, as well as updating material for the catalogue and my book-catalogue, *Phenomonym*. The catalog had been published in the spring, and the book was due for next spring—the updates on it were almost automatic now. There was enough room in the den to display some of my most favorite pieces of art, as well as many archery-related objects, including The Millennium set and many of my yado tools. This was a very concentrated place for me.

More and more of my projects were computer-related now. The network of artisans I was connected to was not restricted to traditional arts, but included capable folks from the high-tech realm as well. Only through a strict process of delegation was I able to keep enough time for my fine art projects.

I had hired a software engineer this summer to develop some special software for me, mostly for the system-intensive graphics I created. I paid him well, but he came to work for me primarily because of my interest in computer systems. I had set up a version of a high-end computer for him to work with, and he had surprised me with his creations—fantastic stuff. I had not realized all that was possible with a mega-system like the one I had set up, but he was showing me, pushing my capabilities. He could have made more money elsewhere but was not interested in fame, power, or riches—he simply enjoyed creating new software that really was able to make use of this huge system.

Frankly, he scared me with some of his surprises. A firm believer in the future of the World Wide Web, he had developed software to monitor the internet and all related networks, allowing someone to tap into e-mail and other communications as easily as the police tapped a phone. This was a scary piece of software, of course, because this product would ruin security for net communications, so I had steered him away from creating other products like it, and had sat on it, except for a little exploration. Sometimes it worried me to have this programmer near my personal system, but he was pushing the boundaries of what could be done on a computer, and he amazed me. His office was separate from the others, and he worked his own hours, showing me his progress when he got excited. I liked him, but his energy was so intense and focused that he scared me sometimes.

My market was a very strange and varied one, including those interested in traditional art, those who liked my modern work, and those who primarily cared about archery-related things. Some of the museum-types didn't appreciate my new directions, and some of those interested in the more modern stuff couldn't seem to appreciate the older work, but there was very little that didn't sell to one market or another. As long as I could follow my imagination I was happy. I bounced back and forth, needing to nourish my roots with my traditional artwork as well as play with the computer-generated artwork and the arrows. I was very happy with the blend, and my body of work was still being enlarged, piece by piece.

The web was becoming an important way to be seen, of course, and there were a series of related sites that displayed my wares. I preferred to separate the sites according to interest, rather than have one site for everything, both to separate my markets and to give the impression of a wealth of work available. The *Millennium* had been featured on the cover of an archery company that dealt with international traditional archery, so I linked the information on the now commercially-available *Millennium* to their site, instead of having it on my own sites. I tried to do that sort of thing as often as I could, and had designed catalogue and web pages at the same time partially with that purpose in mind.

Melissa and I had worked to set up the business so it didn't need our attention very often, and I delegated as much as possible so I would be able to handle my real priorities—family first, art, archery and friends second, everything else third. There were plenty of roses that needing smelling, and we were just the team to do it.

I had recently started making jewelry, and found the intricacies fascinating. Hanna had shown an interest, so I had gotten her involved as well, and she loved it. She was in ninth grade now, in the chorus and doing well in her classes. Each of the kids had their own strengths, and I tried to spend some time with each separately as well as during family time, every day if possible. It was so amazing to watch them grow, to help them over the little hurdles that life sometimes brought, and to show them the things special to me, when they were interested.

We were all going to visit my mother in Florida in a few weeks, our normal Christmas family trip. My brother and two out of three of my sisters would be there at one point or another, and I was looking forward to seeing them again, along with their kids and even a few of their kids' kids. The five of us were spread out all over the country, so we didn't get to see each other often. I was the baby of the family, still considered such even though I was now forty-five—but such is the culture of the South.

Part of the trip was to be a visit to the museum site, where I would again go over the plans with the architects. I had the plans on my system, updated weekly, but, since they used a Windows-based system, I had had to add a Pentium card to my Mac and install their CAD software so I could read and play with the plans. It wasn't very user-friendly, but it was pretty capable software. It would be good to relate their plans to the actual site, to see the beginnings of the physical structure that until now only existed for me in my mind.

There was much to do before we left—business to be conducted, school concerts to attend, deadlines to be met—it would be a crazy time. I laughed—when was there not a crazy time when you were interacting with four lively kids. My bride and I didn't get to spend much time alone, though we made good use of whatever time we did get.

Samantha, my own family's baby, stuck her head in the door, then swooshed herself up on to my lap. Eight years old now and in the third grade, she had the characteristic bounce my kids all seemed to have, even though many would have considered her too big, really, to be popping up on my lap like this.

"Hey, Daddy—help!" She hugged me big.

I laughed. "Help? What'd you do now, Sammy?"

"I didn't do anything, honest. I need your help—c'mon!." She plopped down, taking my hand and pulling me up.

This was it—the big reason we had gone to such extremes to set up at home, instead of being more reasonable and setting up a real office somewhere else. The kids had access to us at all possible times, and they had all developed a sensitivity about when we should or should not be bothered. The studio-barn was off-limits unless I was with them, but otherwise I tried to be here when they needed me. This room was positioned so most all the house traffic passed it, and the pocket door was wide and open.

This was Saturday, so most everyone was home. Jessica was at a sleepover and Hanna was playing at a friend's house, but otherwise we were all about.

"Quiet!" Sam hushed me, pulling me up the stairs. "Be very, very quiet. I want you to see something."

"I thought you needed my help?" Like most children, she knew what would get my attention and what wouldn't, so 'needing help' was a higher priority than 'let me show you something.'

"Shhh." She took me down the hall to Markie's room, slowing as she drew nearer to the door. She put her finger up against her lips to tell me again to be quiet.

I heard sounds of play. She went quietly past the door, stopping at the other side, craning her head to look in the door. I stopped on the near side and peeked around the corner.

Mark was kneeling on the floor with his back to us. He had several action figures lined up against the far wall and was playing some sort of game. The figures weren't from any single story line, but ranged from old *He Man* characters chronologically up through the *Power Rangers*, with many figures I didn't recognize. He would swoop one through the air, making a "keow!" sound, then pick up another figure and have it jump through the air, attacking the first one. Back and forth they would fight, one man throwing another into the corner, then being blown several feet away by some invisible (to us) bomb. A miniature and fantastic war was being fought on our second floor, and it was not a quiet one. Normal stuff for a nine-year old, but Sam was right—the sounds were cute.

I looked over at her. She was holding her hand over her mouth, trying not to laugh. It was my turn to hold my index finger up to my lips.

We watched for a few moments. He had picked up two figures and was doing something with them in his lap. I cupped my hands at an angle around my mouth to try to redirect the sound and made a "keow!" sound of my own.

Markie jerked his head up, looked left, then right, then left again.

For all the world he seemed as though he was trying to figure out which of his toys had made the new sound.

After a few seconds of this Sam burst into laughter, then ran away, down the stairs two at a time. Mark turned around and looked at me, then got a sheepish grin on his face. I went in to help him play for a time, a special time.

Moments like these were important to me, tending to be the things that stuck most vividly in my memory. We played together for an hour or so, and the world was eventually saved from the bad guys, if you could stretch your definition of which characters were the bad guys just a little bit. When we finished I helped him arrange the figures on their shelf, then he ran down to the kitchen for a snack.

I enjoyed remembering special times given to me by my family, memories kept like many jewels picked up along a long path.

Although she was fourteen now, I remembered when Jessica had brought her bicycle to me, asking me to please take off her training wheels. Skeptical, I refused, telling her she should practice for a few more weeks. She was not that old, then, and I worried about her safety. She went away, angry with her father.

An hour later she returned on a bicycle with only two wheels, showing me her expertise and control. She demonstrated her cycling prowess for me, forcing me to admit her skill level. While I was more than a little pissed, I had to concede her ability, capitulating, removing her training wheels.

She had gone to a neighbor's house up our little road and returned on a too-big borrowed bike just to show me I had been wrong. I had to admire her tenacity if not her strict obedience—the training wheels were, after all, still on her own bicycle.

She proved me wrong that day, and never had as much as a skinned knee on that bike. Unfortunately for me though, her tenacity and love of the bicycle meant I never would get to teach any of my other children how to ride. Before I knew they even wanted to learn, she would teach them, one by one, taking away my joy of watching them rolling their first wobbly yards after my hand left the back of the seat.

This kind of cooperation brought my children together as playmates instead of just as siblings—my bunkins were close to one another, a team.

*The soft-lead pencil smoothly scraped a curved line down the rag paper, turning into Melissa's beautiful neck.*

*She was turned, looking to my extreme left, Samantha beside her. They were juxtaposed so this portrait would show both their profiles, and I labored to place each stroke perfectly.*

*Their features were so similar, my wife and my eight-year-old baby girl. When you took into account Sam's physical immaturity, you could see how much she was going to look like her mother, the most beautiful woman I had ever known. Missy had fixed Sam's hair so it matched her own, which delighted the little twinkler—it had already matched in light blonde color, mid-back length, and fine texture. Their noses and cheekbones were the same shape, they had the same complexions, and their blue eyes matched, a light blue to contrast with my own darker blue. They wore similar outfits, made to show off their necks so I could capture the shape of their throats.*

*One of the most exciting things about this drawing was the chance to express my wife's mature features with the roundish innocence of eight-year-old Samantha. Each profile taken separately would have stood alone, but only as a portrait—together, though, they would express a timelessness of the female spirit. They made a picture of human continuity.*

*I started shading with Samantha, capturing the shadows on the side of her face, trying to finish her as quickly as possible. She wanted to sit for this portrait, but had a bad case of ants in her little pants.*

Just before Christmas break we visited the school for Hanna's choral recital. It was held at the elementary school, a small building with small classes, a place where we were not strangers. We enjoyed working on projects for the classes, as well as participating in Career Day, or even just visiting once in a while.

Everything was decorated for the holidays, and the excitement level of the kids was explosive. They were running through the halls to the bathrooms, making sure they were ready—some of them were even wearing a little makeup, perhaps for the first time. They were hyper and ready for the big extravaganza, followed by a vacation, and we all knew how they felt—we were ready too. This was Thursday night, and we would leave for our trip Monday morning, another beautiful fall season behind us.

The recital was held in the cafeteria. It wasn't the kind of event that drew large crowds—mainly families of the kids—so didn't warrant setting up in the gym. The chorus drew from the middle school as well as the elementary, and was made up of a fluctuating group of about twenty kids, mostly female. There was a three-tiered platform set up at the end of the room with the audience sitting in folding chairs around the lunch tables. We had to be careful to pick the right seats, because the director always had the piano set up directly in front of the singers so she could conduct, and we wanted to make sure we could see and video without having to move about. I knew where Hanna would be standing.

I liked to get there early so I could watch the kids bustle about. I knew most of them, some since they were bitty things, and I knew their hierarchies. There was a small group made up of the popular kids, another for the brains, still another of the kids who joined only to be with their friends, and the final group who, while perhaps not especially bright or pretty, could still sing better than most, and knew it. They were the only ones who took this event very seriously, perhaps even hoping for a singing career someday, and we appreciated their dream. Hanna liked to sing and practiced at home, but never settled down enough to really develop her vocal control.

The kids gathered in the hall and filed in on the director's command, filling up the top tier, then the middle (Hanna near the end between Madeline and Jo, two close friends), then the bottom. We had all hushed, then created a buzz as we each saw our own child or children. Hanna was smiling, whispering in her friends' ears, and generally refusing to settle down, but that was to be expected.

The director had tried to pick a range of holiday songs to both express the holiday spirit and not bore the kids, so there were some modern songs added to the mix. These children were maturing at wildly different rates, some becoming little adults, and it would have been impossible to pick a selection of songs that didn't embarrass one child or another. It was easy to tell when the singers thought they were doing something lame by the way they grimaced and tried to hide their faces, but I could only laugh—they were so darn cute.

As I watched Hanna sing, her hair all permed and kinky, her expression sometimes solemn (finally), I was suddenly reminded of her when she had been only one or two years old. She and I were in an old truck I had at the time, sitting parked at the house, having a disagreement over something she wanted that I wouldn't let her have. We weren't going anywhere, and I didn't remember why we were in the truck, but I did remember her standing up next to the door in only her diaper, looking at me with her chubby face. Her bottom lip was pouted, and a little tear was running down her chewy little cheek. She looked so very sad. She wasn't saying anything more, her part of the argument over, but she just looked so hurt and disappointed. I remember holding her, crying with her, never wanting to let her go, feeling her little spirit, so trusting and pure.

I had wanted so much for this Bunkin, this special sweet soul, and now she was growing up, literally, right before my eyes.

Her little face I remembered then merged into her maturing face I saw now, and I couldn't help crying, knowing I couldn't ever hold this little lady the same way I had then, that she was well on her way to becoming a grown-up, a lady. Missy handed me a Kleenex, laying a gentle hand on my arm.

All the kids were spending the night other places on Saturday, saying good-bye to friends they wouldn't see for a little while. Melissa and I were looking forward to a rare evening alone, especially since the whole family would be crowded together for the long RV trip.

By late afternoon everyone was gone. I fixed a little supper for us while she did some packing and we ate by the light of a kerosene lantern in the early dark. We talked about the route we would take, about travel activities for the kids, about leaving the business—small things, necessary things.

After we ate and cleaned up we watched a video, *Benny & Joon*, one of our favorites. We sipped our wine as we cuddled on the couch in the darkened room, comfortable and happy.

I had my back against the cushions, nice and warm. She was laying with her back to my front, my arms and legs wrapped around her, her head almost on a level with mine.

I nibbled her right ear, breathing slightly into it as her mood deepened. Her ears were funny things—if I tried to breathe into them when she wasn't ready it would tickle her, and that was definitely not what I wanted to do. I worked around its perimeter, using just the tips of my teeth to gently scrape the edges of her outer ear, working down to the lobe.

"Hey! There's a movie on here, y'know."

"I know—so watch it."

"I'm sort of being distracted."

"That's okay—I'll stay right back here, out of the way, just watching the movie."

"Right."

I explored some more, working down to the base of her neck. She groaned softly and I laughed, biting down a little harder, pinching the muscle. She screamed a little and twisted away from my bite.

"So much for the movie," she said, using the remote.

"Movie? You wanted to watch a movie?"

"Very much I want to watch this movie..."

"Oh, I'm sorry—should I leave you alone?" I pouted for her benefit.

"Better idea. Why don't we take a little break?"

"Sure!" I said, starting to jump up. She had my vote.

It was a while before she got to finish her movie.

*My first computer was a Timex Sinclair, a little baby of a thing with only 2k of ram and a plastic membrane keyboard. It connected to a small black-and-white television and stored its programs on a cheap cassette recorder.*

*It worked well by our low standards of way back when, and I was later even able to add a simple word processor, even though the printer only printed text on a four-inch wide roll of thermal paper.*

*I learned a lot from that little thing. It had BASIC language built into it, implemented simply and well, and that somehow gave me insight into the way computers "thought." I learned when and why it was "thinking" and the things it "liked" or "hated."*

*Now I would sit down to work on my Macintosh, the multiple processors, drives, monitors, printers—as well as the keyboard, trackball, drawing tablet, and other peripherals surrounding me on three sides. I would feel the hum of all this well-powered equipment coordinated to work together, to work in sync with all its parts and with me to produce amazing and complex things. I was the conductor, all the musicians, and the audience as well, sometimes, the computer-instruments joining me in rapport.*

*I understood this system as well as I had little that Timex Sinclair, even though it was hundreds of times more powerful. I knew how to ask it to do things we couldn't have imagined a few years ago, working between all its components to perform for me, expanding out on the network for needed resources, even flowing out onto the Internet when necessary.*

*In order for us to work together my equipment and I needed this understanding. We reflected each other.*

*I knew there were those out there that fought their computers, treating them like inanimate objects. I always wondered how they got anything done.*

*A bad attitude could freeze the electron flow as quickly as a pulled plug.*

We discussed many things on the down leg of our trip, including business.

Melissa had her own version of my idea notebook that she kept updated with current and future business opportunities and thoughts. She was the real reason I was successful—if it had been left up to me, I would have been content to make things and then just pass them out the door, ready for the next project. She managed everything, a real talent, notebook ready to record any and all thoughts.

I'm the first to admit that I don't understand money. It's a tool for me, a way to open doors to larger and larger possibilities. I knew I wouldn't be able to afford my high-tech toys and tools without her oversight and management, and I appreciated it. I knew things would be different if I didn't know where my next meal was to appear, but because of this lady I didn't have to worry about it—I was doing all right.

Before she handled my affairs I was making a fair amount of money through the agent I used, the one she had originally worked for, but not really hanging on to any of it. Somehow it evaporated, just rose up into the sky.

I remembered when my mother tried to get me to be responsible about money by opening a savings account with me. I was only about nine or so, but I remembered how excited I was, and how much I wanted to save my money.

I had a brand new five-dollar bill that I had earned by mowing the lawn. When I got it in my hot little hands I was very careful with it, making sure it was kept flat in a book when I wasn't at home. I studied the engraved details of it, the clean, intricate lines, the little squiggly red and blue fibers imbedded in the paper, the sheer beauty and cohesiveness of the design. I had something special here, and I was going to be very careful with it. This wasn't a tool for me but a significant object all its own, and I was going to keep it forever. No Fanner-Fifty toy guns, no comic books, no coonskin caps, no candy, but just the first in a tall stack-to-be of special bills in denominations of all sizes.

I carefully memorized all the details—the portrait of Abraham Lincoln, the series number, the seal of the city where it was printed, the Secretary's name, all of it. I spent special effort to memorize the serial number, because it was the thing that made my five-dollar bill unique. I treasured that bill.

My mother talked me into depositing the money in the neighborhood bank, convincing me that it would be safe there. This was in the days before there were such things as malls, and we lived miles from downtown.

Edgewood Avenue was where we did most of our shopping. It was an amazing place, covering four long blocks on both sides. In the middle of the last block was the bank we used. Only five blocks from my home, I walked there with my grandmother, Nanny. She lived across the street and over two houses, so I saw her frequently.

Nanny also had a chore at the bank, needing to cash a check, so we went together, she standing in line behind me at the teller's window. I had my new-ish savings account passbook with me, given as much care as my money, and handed both to the teller so she could validate the deposit of my five-dollar bill. When she returned the book and I had checked the entry that represented my money, I stepped aside to wait for my grandmother. She cashed her check and I watched in horror as the teller counted out her money, laying my five-dollar bill on top.

I had misunderstood the reality of money, and that was the last time I remember caring about money as an actual thing. I know the concern I had for that physical five-dollar bill should have been replaced by that neat entry in my savings passbook, but it never happened, then or later.

Melissa and I were discussing the Internet as it related to our business, the children asleep in the back as we barreled down I-26 over and down to I-95 in our sealed environment. She felt strongly about the value of the web, and wanted us to become a major presence, if there were a way. She was pitching it to me—she didn't need my approval, of course, but knew I would only whole-heartedly give my creative abilities to a project that excited me.

"Okay," she said, "Point one: The way the world works at this time, an advertiser will try to reach anyone who might possibly need, want, or be slightly interested in their product. They'll spend as much time, energy, and resources as they need to build a new market, or to gain market share. Right?"

"Sure."

"Okay. Point two. Computers. The new operating systems are able to anticipate us a little bit, right? I mean, if you do something one way all the time, the software is starting to anticipate the way you work, and will occasionally suggest an action for you—you see it all the time, and it's only going to become more capable as computers become faster and cheaper." She was riding shotgun, sitting sideways to talk to me—it was my shift.

"Of course, Babe. I've read enough to know that the newer system upgrades are heading more and more in that direction."

"Anyway," she said, "there are things they call agents. They're little software bits you can assign tasks to, like searching the 'net at night to research something."

"I know."

"Anyway, I was thinking: Since we can assume this trend will only get stronger as computers get faster and software gets more powerful, we need to project where this will lead."

"Project away, m'dear."

Okay.  Point three.  If these agents are watching everything we do, including everything we look at on the 'net, then isn't it possible they'll learn a lot of the things we're interested in?  You know, the kind of music we like, who we e-mail, the kind of catalogue stuff we order, all that stuff."

"Okay."

"Okay."  She was in her element now.  "Isn't it possible, then, that if the agents know you're interested in say, the group Crash Test Dummies, but only the albums that have banjo, won't they be able to notify you of the instant a new qualifying album hits the street?"

"Sure, why not?  Actually, they'd probably know before it was for sale."

"Okay.  What's that going to do to advertising?"

"In what way?"

"If, say, you're interested in something—widgets, for example, and a little guy in South Africa goes on the 'net selling handmade left-handed indigenous widgets, you would know of it immediately.  See?"

"Okay..."

"Okay, so in the old days, like now, that guy wouldn't have been able to find any of the maybe two hundred people in the whole world that care about these widgets, but with these agents, even the little guy will have instant worldwide exposure, and only to the people who care."

"Hmm."

"Indeed," she said.  "So that makes this little guy working in his garage in South Africa on an advertising par with Mr.  United Worldwide Widgets, based in Big City, USA, right?"

"Right, as long as he can keep up with the demand."

"His problem, and one every supplier would love to have, right?"

"Right."

"So if there is a demand for something, the creator of it will know almost immediately without having to go through all the crap that developers and manufacturers and distributors and ad agencies have to go through now.  He'll know what his market is!"

"Hmm..."

"So now you have two things, a medium that supports the little guy as well as the big guy, which means that innovations will be speeded up, and a medium that will always show what is available, anywhere in the world.  The only reason for advertising will be to create a new demand, and the 'net will be filling that need too, at least partially, through contacting those that might be interested.

"This means we won't have to worry about unemployment as much, either, because there will be more chances for more people to create the things they want to, instead of working for companies that might downsize them at the smallest excuse. If nobody out there wants to buy their product, then at least they will have tried, and they'll also have been put in contact with other people that share their interests."

"But," I said, "isn't that what we're doing already? Do you want me to see about developing the software or something?" Interesting idea, I thought, I'll bet he could do it. Of course, this sounded like the potential beginnings of Big Brother, but we were in a good position to counter that.

"No, that's not what I meant, except that the new guy you hired might have some ideas, too. I know we are already as exposed on the web as we can be—I just want to we can take advantage of this new direction."

I lit my pipe. After thinking for a few minutes, I used the tip of the stem of it to move the moustache hairs away from my lips, shifting them aside, like a single-toothed comb.

"I can't see anything wrong with the idea, Lover. Interesting times, neh?"

She pulled my braid as she leaned over to kiss my cheek.

"Oh," I said. "Speaking of work.

"That new girl making the alternate arrows doesn't seem to be catching on very quickly. What should we do?" I had added a new line of arrows that I though of as alternatives to my standard product—three new lines really. The first was Authentic Shafts, recreating arrows that duplicated those of old cultures, some Native American, some European, some Asian. The second was Spirit Arrows, for those who wanted to be buried with their tackle. These matched special bows made with very stringent requirements, including the use of only natural materials harvested under only proper conditions. The emphasis so far seemed to be on arrows decorated with white, predominantly, and shaping the points and nocks out of materials like jade and turquoise are what had gotten me interested in making jewelry. The third type of arrow were the Presentation Grade, arrows that had escutcheon plates, or precious metal fittings, or even handpainted scenes. These arrows all required someone who paid a great deal of attention to spiritual details as well as artistic ones.

"Oops—sorry. She seemed like a good match. What's the problem?"

"Well, technically she's doing okay, but her attitude isn't quite right. She doesn't understand the special nature of these arrows, maybe. It's kind of hard to explain to someone what makes them so special. Maybe I can have another talk with her when we get back."

"Would she be better with the regular stuff?"

"Maybe—maybe I can switch her with someone else. She has talent."

"Let me know what I can do, okay?"

"Sure, Darlin'. Have I told you lately I love you?"

"Not near enough."

"I love you."


*There is an elegance in total expression far out of proportion to the effort it consumes.*

*When you involve yourself in the creation of something you love, you lose track of time. It doesn't matter what the activity is—making an arrow, performing archery, painting, photography, playing with the kids, loving your spouse, driving a vehicle, raking the yard. If it's a job that needs to be done, it's a job that needs to be done well.*

*If you are not happy doing it, it will not be done well.*

*I remember a time in college that I took a job working for a house painter. His contract was to paint houses in a new subdivision as soon as they were finished. He had eight people working for him, including me.*

*We would "chase" the builders, ready to move as soon as they were finished, four people to a crew—two inside, two outside. I was originally assigned to paint inside window frames, and I enjoyed it. There was an art to it. Using the proper brush laden with just the right amount of paint, the brush is "laid in" to the "mutton bar," as it's called. The brush is drawn along the wood strips at just the right speed, leaving a smoothly painted surface with very clean lines. There was always a rush, but the goal was to do a perfect job as quickly as possible. If the paint were applied to the glass instead of the wood it would have to be trimmed with a razor blade after drying, wasting time.*

*We got into a crunch and I was reassigned to stain exterior walls— the outside crews were falling behind. The walls were unusual to me, constructed of exterior plywood with a squarely-recessed space at even intervals, 3/8" wide and running all the way from the top of the wall down to the base. These little recesses were a bitch to stain, narrow and square, constructed so it was difficult to get enough stain inside the groove without getting too much everywhere else. It was a time-consuming process to stain each one of these grooves correctly, and that was my assignment—that and nothing else.*

*After a few days I approached my boss with the idea to use a hand-sprayer to stain these grooves. Similar to the sprayers used to apply weed killer, they are pumped by hand to build the pressure necessary to push out the stain out a narrow tip at the end of a wand a few feet long, bent at the tip. He was skeptical, but rented one for me to try.*

*By the end of the day I had my rhythm. I would lean a piece of scrap plywood up under the bottom lip of the wall to redirect the runoff onto the grassless yard, then hold the tip of the sprayer up to the top of the groove. Holding the trigger I would run the tip down to the bottom, releasing stain all the way down. After checking quickly to make sure it had been done correctly, I would move to the next groove.*

*It worked so well that he let me go at the end of the week, because we had caught up to the contractor—we were out of houses.*

Our Christmas had been wonderful. It had been an unusually warm winter, even for Florida, and the water fronting the lake house was still warm enough to be able to enjoy a swim. We were packed to go home, and it was almost time to leave—a great afternoon spent on the porch watching the kids swimming around, splashing one another.

It had been good to see my family—it didn't really happen enough. I loved to watch my mother with my bunkins, especially at this time of year—she enjoyed them so much.

One of the things I always had to remember to get my mother was a CARE package of Twizzlers. This year there were three packs, two red and one black, and I remembered thinking that those three packages of candy should have lasted her for quite some time. Unfortunately I had forgotten to factor in the rest of the family, and the candy had been gone within a few hours—sucked up. I had to laugh, though, when I saw my mother's reaction to her now-gone candy, because I hadn't seen her pout like that for many years past—it's always the little things, isn't it?

We had stayed at the lake during this visit, on property that my parents had bought in 1938. The other branches of the family tree had stayed at various places around Jacksonville, but we had stayed here, driving the hour north when we needed to go into town. I heard the special Woodstock windchimes Melissa had given me for Christmas—I had hung them on the porch for our time here. They seemed to fit in this place, too.

In all the world, this was the place I thought of as my home, no matter where else I lived. The original structure here had been and old farm house, but my parents had replaced it in 1988 with this modern log cabin, fieldstone fireplace and all. It was a very nice place, kept now mostly for situations just like this, but it wasn't the house that was so special to me.

Somehow the air here smelled like air should smell, the sandy earth crumbled and shifted under my bare feet in a subtle way that was just right, somehow. When I spent the day here my hair was warm, felt like it had soaked up as much energy as it could possibly hold, saving it somehow for later use like it was a rechargeable battery. Thinking of that reminded me of the Native American symbol for wisdom, braids long enough to touch the earth. I felt that my braid might touch the earth someday, and if it did it would be here.

I missed this place, especially the water. My older brother had taught me how to swim when I was three, right here, and I was never quite so content as when I was sitting down on the sandy bottom of this lake, playing with the little fish. I had always wished I could hold my breath longer—I tried scuba gear, but it just didn't feel the same. Minnesota may lay claim to ten thousand lakes, but Florida has over thirty thousand—and those are just the ones that had names. The smell, feel, and taste of this water was unique and perfect for me.

One of the reasons this had been a good place for us to stay this trip had been the meeting with the architects, just a half-hour away. It was good to stand on the land where the Archery Guild Museum would be erected one day soon. All the museum plans had been approved by the committee, with minor modifications, and I was able to walk the property, visually placing the museum firmly in my mind's eye, seeing where the outdoor ranges would be set up, admiring the sheer expanse of the property.

There was extra land here, and my secret hope was that one day there might be a community evolving, a community of archers. I still believed there were no more helpful or conscientious people anywhere, as a group, and knew this would be a good place to live and share. I fully expect intentional communities to make a comeback when the Baby Boomers like me age, and it would be about damn time. It's something we never should have given up.

*While we were at the museum site Melissa and I had shot our bows, along with Hanna and Samantha. Hanna was left-eyed so she shot her bow left-handed, and little Sam was just about to outgrow the Little Bear bow, the tiny fifteen-pounder she loved to shoot. Melissa was shooting a self-bow, a hickory recurve that used wood that had grown with a natural curve to it. This shooting time was sort of a personal ceremony for us, our own dedication of this land.*

*I watched them shoot for a while, especially my wife. As I watched her I could feel my own chest muscles expanding as she drew, my own back muscles contracting. I felt her holding the bow at full draw, felt her release—it was like I was the one shooting, almost like I was seeing through her eyes. I had never been this close to someone, and watching her shoot made me cherish our connection. This was a new dimension to archery for me, made even more empathic by the little ones' attempts to shoot straight.*

Once everything had been packed in the RV and unplugged in the house, we said good-bye to the lake for another season, coming back to town for one last day before heading back to Kentucky.

We went to Mom's house for a while, then went out to lunch—my mom likes to eat out these days, at least when there's company.

It's difficult for me to realize she's eighty-one now, because she looks the way I've always remembered her—the same sense of humor, the same love of card games, the same everything. I never really wondered about that before, but it's true. She had trouble with her knees, but that had been the case for a long time, and her eyes, if anything, were better than before because of new laser surgery technologies.

After lunch Melissa and I took Samantha to do a little shopping. We borrowed Mom's car and I stopped to fill it up at her usual place. The station was a short block south of the intersection of Normandy Boulevard and Cassat Avenue, a major local four lane road. Cassat is oriented north and south, and we were to go north on it until we got to the entrance to I-10, just five or six blocks away, then east to I-95.

The curves where I-10 merged with I-95 had fascinated me all my life. I remembered that I would sometimes walk over from Five Points, the area where my family's church was, and stand where I could watch that road, facing west. It simply amazed me this was the very spot where I-10 started, stretching across the whole width of the country, all the way to the Pacific. It was the same feeling I would have when I stood on the beach and watched the ocean, thinking about all the wondrous places far out there. The difference was that I-10 was on land, and that made those far away places much more real somehow. I could walk, if I had to—not very practical, but interesting to ponder.

After I paid for the gas Melissa remembered she wanted something else and went inside for it. I started the car, waiting. She got in and buckled up, checked Sam's belt, then gave me the go-ahead. I rolled forward, looking for a opening onto Cassat. When I saw an opening I pulled out speedily, making it cleanly into the left lane before having to stop at the Normandy light, first in line.

A late-model Ford pulled up on our right. I glanced over and saw a large man staring at my wife, apparently oblivious to anything else. I didn't call her attention to it—she drew stares all the time, from boys just out of puberty way on up to older men. She was an amazing, attractive woman.

It tickled me sometimes to watch young men stumble over themselves when Melissa was present. Sometimes I would stand back and watch her getting this attention, somehow made more special by her innocence of the havoc she wreaked.

Getting a little impatient about the light, I glanced over to the driver of the Ford again—he was still staring. His focus was odd—he didn't seem to be quite aware of the world.

Something about him made me feel very uneasy—perhaps he was drunk or drugged. As comfortable as I was with the energies of other people, I had come to know that if there were an unawareness or lack of focus to a person they became slightly unreal to me, sort of fuzzy, certainly unpredictable.

Finally, the light changed. I moved ahead, and when I noticed the Ford hadn't moved yet I quickly pulled over to the right lane. This guy made me nervous, and I thought I would feel better without him next to me. I needed to be in the right lane to get up onto I-10 in a few blocks, anyway.

When I looked back I saw and felt he was angry now—perhaps he was upset that I jumped ahead of him, or perhaps, if he were drunk, he took offense that I deprived him of his fixation, whatever it was. His car jumped ahead in the rear view mirror, weaving slightly. This guy had to be drunk. I reached for the cell phone, then realized I hadn't brought it. Damn!

He was coming up fast, speeding to catch up to me. I had no idea how dangerous he might be to me or my family, but I did know that there was potential for danger here.

All I could do now was to watch him and get out of his way as quickly as possible, then report him. I sped up, trying to make the entrance ramp as quickly as possible. He was gaining on us. I thought perhaps that if I could lose him in one calculated maneuver it would get us out of his way.

As I approached the ramp I measured distances and speed, careful not to put on my blinker—I didn't want to give this guy any chances.

He was coming up too fast. I turned onto the ramp, tires screaming. Melissa screamed, upsetting Samantha.

"What are you doing?" She hadn't noticed the encounter. Sam was crying now, not understanding.

I quickly told Melissa about the situation, and as she turned around to look behind her, we both saw the Ford careening around the corner of the curve, grazing his left-rear fender on a light pole in the process. I couldn't believe he made that turn.

"I want to call 9-1-1, but I left the damn phone in the RV."

"Oh, no, no—I picked it up!" She reached over the back of the seat and tightened Sam's seat belt, talking to her while she did it, calming her. She turned back around and reached to the floor for her bag, still talking to Sam. She found the phone, yanked out the antenna, then held down the nine key. The operator answered.

As she reported the situation I increased my speed again. We were well on the Interstate now, four lanes going in each direction across a wide median, and he was definitely trying to catch me, weaving in and out of his lane. He sideswiped a VW bug, one of the older tiny ones, pushing it from the second lane into the third, then came on again.

I told Missy about the crash and she told the 9-1-1 operator.

I considered my options.

I should be able to out-drive this guy if he was drunk, and could certainly handle him if we were in a face-to-face confrontation, whether he was drunk or not.

My first priority was my family's safety, my second priority was the safety of everybody else on the road, my third was the safety of Mom's car.

I thought perhaps that if he lost sight of our car he might lose interest, so as I passed an eighteen-wheeler I shifted over in the its lane. I looked out the side-mirror to keep track of the drunk's position. He was coming up fast. I checked the third lane, the one to my left—it was clear.

Perhaps I could shift over there, then drop back beside the truck, out of the drunk's sight, then slow down until I was clear, changing lanes to move behind the big trailer, gradually making a big circle around it. That should work. We passed the Edgewood Avenue exit, too far away to do me any good. Stockton Street was next, I thought. I wished I was in my own car.

The drunk was coming up very quickly, and I shifted to the third lane, making sure it was safe, then drifted back to try to hide from him. I dropped back more as I saw the tip of his hood show in front of the truck, keeping even with the cab for a few moments. When I saw him speed on by, I tried to drop back further, but there was a Caddy coming up quickly, not wanting to give way.

The fourth lane, the far left, was blocked, so I stepped on the brake, trying to make the Caddy give me some room—he was actually forcing me ahead, keeping me too far forward! The driver leaned on his horn, and I saw the drunk jerk his head around, spotting me and swerving. If he had just been a little farther ahead, he wouldn't have seen me or heard the horn.

Trapped now, I slowed down more, and the Caddy swung over to the next lane, thoroughly pissed. When I was clear I swerved far over to the first lane, hoping against hope my move could still be successful. I didn't see the drunk.

The Stockton Street exit was on me and I had to move quickly. I drifted on to the ramp just as the Ford smashed into my left side, forcing both of us to take the curve much too widely. We separated from the Ford, moving farther right, tighter into the curve, then hit the guard rail, bouncing back out to the left, sliding across the ramp almost sideways, smashing into the Ford again. His extra weight was keeping me from maintaining control, and we were moving much too fast.

*I regained consciousness groggily, heard an engine racing, sirens piercing. I looked to my left and saw the Ford on its back, rear wheels spinning at high speed. I moved my head to the right, feeling something warm and wet on that side of my face. I reached up to wipe it off and felt an agonizingly sharp pain in my right arm. I couldn't reach my face, so I turned my whole head further to try to see with my left eye.*

*I saw an ambulance, attendants already at my mother's car. I tried to* move, to get to them somehow, but another attendant stopped me, pushed me firmly back onto the ground.

"Just lie back, man. You're bleeding like a stuck pig."

"My wife! My baby!"

"They're being taken care of. You'll all be at St. Vincent's real quick— just don't fight me! Just try to stay awake, okay?"

I lost consciousness slowly. It was like falling asleep, but without the control I needed to wake up, to get to them. I had to, though, I had to.

"St. Vincent's Hospital?"

"Yeah, man."

"I was born at St. Vincent's."

As I fell down into the darkness, I heard someone scream, "Her hands! Look at her hands!"

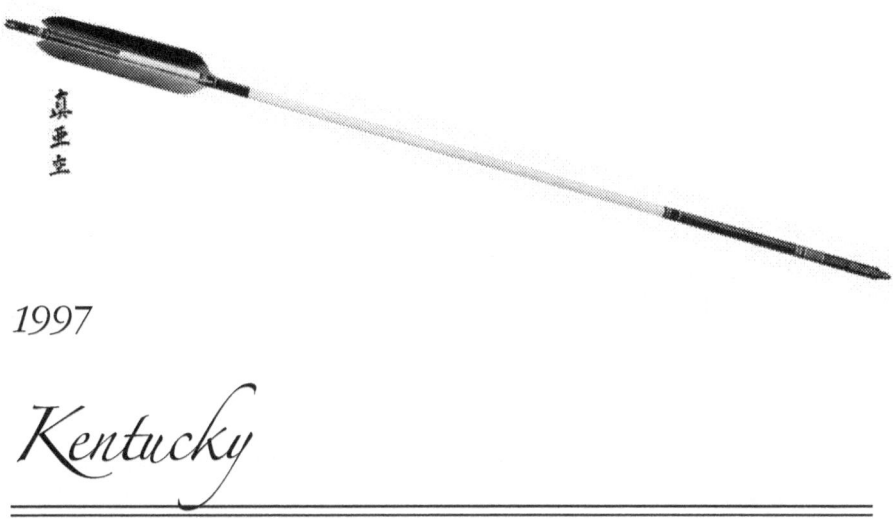

1997

# Kentucky

*I stared into the flames, watching the mixing interplay of their reds, oranges, yellows, and whitish edge colors rise over my head into the darkness, merging together higher and higher, sending sparks up to join the stars above me.*

*There were enough logs piled in the burning circle to burn tall and brightly, a pyre to honor my loved ones, a message to whatever spirits would listen. The coals were growing ever hotter, glowing a luminescent light and heat against my face in the still-cold March.*

*I lit this fire to hold my gaze, lit it night after night when there was no more I could do for my family that day. The constant I held on to now was the impermanence of the flames, for the other solid things didn't mean much to me in my grief.*

*I think I understood the parable of the lost sheep more completely now, for I could only concentrate on my losses—the ninety-nine sheep left were not very much in my thoughts, I am sorry to say.*

My days were spent at the Albert B. Chandler Medical Center in Lexington with Melissa and Sam, nights in my burning circle. It was the best hospital in the state, performing research in critical-care and other major fields, with doctors, researchers, and staff I trusted. If there was help anywhere, I thought, it was here.

I had gotten a gouged scalp in the accident, as well as a wound in my right arm, but it had looked much worse than it was. I did lose a lot of blood quickly—that's why I lost consciousness—but had sustained no permanent damage.

Jessica, Hanna, and Markie were being cared for at our house by Granny Rebecca, their maternal grandmother from Ohio. I had tried to take care of my children by myself, to share our grief while supporting their daily needs, but it had been too much for me, even though they helped as much as they could. Jessica, especially, had helped, taking charge of the household duties, making sure the others were fed and clothed, becoming a de facto mother, but I had still asked Rebecca to stay with us so I wouldn't have to worry about depending on a teenager.

Perhaps it was unfair of me to usurp her new-found rôle, but I needed to concentrate on Missy and Sam and didn't want to be distracted by Jessica's learning curve. They all respected my space, understood my focus—even Jessica. The only condition I made to Rebecca before she came to stay with us was to respect Jessie's mom-like status—she was blossoming right before my eyes, concerned about her mom and sister, but showing how adult a fifteener could be, and I felt it was important to allow her this blossoming time. Rebecca seemed to understand.

I had charged the Business Manager of my office to handle the several levels of our business so I wouldn't have to be distracted, and I thanked God again for Melissa's choice of capable and dependable people. I didn't have to work now, and I wondered more than once how those with regular jobs managed in a situation like this—how they could go to an office every day when they were desperately needed elsewhere.

*Phenomonym* had come out on time. In fact, the notoriety of our situation had generated an unbelievable demand for it, and a reprint had been ordered.

*I sat by the hospital bed, my left hand on her little thigh. The things that had been her hands were swathed in multiple layers of bandages, great balls of white that ended just below the IV shunt in her forearm. Her head was wrapped as well, the baby-fine blonde hair shaved under it, ready for another operation.*

*The walls of the room were covered with drawings from her third-grade classmates wishing her well, and I made sure there were always bright flowers where she could see them, if she would just open her eyes.*

*I faced the decorated headboard as I sat next to her, cross-legged on the armless chair. As I moved my hand up to rest on her upper chest just below her collarbone, I closed my eyes, calming myself. Extending my senses, I tried to feel the little Samantha that still lived inside.*

*The touch of her skin was so familiar that I knew she was there, knew my baby would have to be all right. The texture of her, the vibration that said her name was so very strong.*

*If only she would move.*

*It was difficult to explain what I was looking for in the touch of Sam's skin. It was the texture of it, to be sure, but more than that, just as it was more than feeling her bones or her muscles underneath the skin, more even than feeling the warmth of her. There was something more like a magnetic field or even one of an electrical or spiritual nature—something that said "Here I am—I am your Samantha."*

*Scared, I remembered holding my father's hand in his casket. I could feel his energy, his own psychic nature, even after he was gone, and that memory worried me now. I had no doubt that if you had closed my eyes and led me to his side I would have been able to recognize him from just the touch of his hand—but he had left, never to return. If I could feel him then as I felt my daughter now, how did I know my Sam would live again, play again, hug me again? Could I trust this touch to tell me she was okay? If my father could still be felt after his death, how could I trust what I felt now?*

*I "entered my own closet," as it says in Matthew, praying the Lord's Prayer for my little one, meditating on each phrase, trying to feel it in me and through me to her.*

*I touched with a healing hand, the same touch I had used on all the children when they had fevers. Now, as I had then, I would try to protect their little bodies while a part of them would fight until the fever broke.*

*I knew the healing power was there, knew it knew no bounds, knew she would be well. I envisioned her head, hands, and heart whole and well, saw her bouncing around me again, happy. If I could only grasp her, hold her from falling into the abyss, somehow awaken her enough to help me to help her...*

*I tried not to get frustrated when she didn't awaken, tried not to panic, tried to be a pure conduit for the healing I knew would come, tried to be calm—but something had changed. Whatever power I normally had access to seemed to be shut off, and no amount of kyudo or yado practice centered me enough to bring it back.*

*Something was blocking the flow I normally felt, the awareness I had grown used to. I could still focus to the front, but was wearing some sort of psychic blinders that required me to focus tightly, too tightly.*

*I was fighting the part of me that had closed down, some injury that had not been physical.*

I got up after a while and went to Melissa's side—she needed her own special care in her own room. It was a break for me to walk from one place to the other, and was about the only time I took to eat something or go to the bathroom.

Most of the time her eyes were open, but her catatonia was no less severe than Samantha's. We were lucky today, those of us who watched over her, because she wasn't having the shaking fits or muscular rigidity that occasionally plagued her—I could only hope that was a sign she was recovering. I don't think the doctors were as truthful with me as they should have been about her prognosis, so I had come to trust my own feelings and hopes.

Melissa had not had injuries as severe as Sam's, although she had lost a lot of blood. Before collapsing she had grabbed Sam up in her arms, unable to do anything but hold her as her life's blood had drained from her head and her poor little hands. Ignoring her own injuries, she must have taken in the pure horror of her baby's pain, perhaps made more horrible by seeing me lying there, motionless on the ground. Whatever she saw or felt had affected her deeply enough to throw her into a coma she had not been able to escape.

I didn't want to touch her the same way I touched Sam, because deep in my heart I didn't know whether she blamed me for the accident the same way I blamed myself. Sometimes I thought if she awakened and found me touching her that she would scream in terror, wanted to be as far away from me as possible. It had been my job to protect my family and I had failed as miserably as if I had attacked them myself. Melissa's escape into unconsciousness only added to my guilt.

I did touch her, though, because my need to heal her outweighed my fear of her opinion of me. I needed her—we should both be at Sam's side, supporting each other through these hard times. Sometimes I was angry with her for leaving me alone, almost as if she had chosen to escape this way, but I never told anyone that, ashamed of the feeling. I ached for her, and I cried for her—my precious lady, my strength. I wished so hard that she could forgive me, come back to me.

I talked to her often, many times a day. I told her where she was, what her physical condition was, how Sam was, how the bunkins were, what was happening in the rest of the family, in the business, whatever I could think to tell her. I had always treated my babies as though they were competent individuals that could be trusted with truth and responsibility. I felt it was important I treat my wife the same way now, that I ask her questions I knew she would want to answer as a caring, responsible adult.

I had made a list of the things I could remember that interested her, bugged her, anything—anything that might get a rise out of her, make her laugh, get her to remember. I consulted the list often and tried to add to it as often as I could, to make it as varied and far-ranging as possible.

If she could hear me, I wanted to give her brain as much to feed on as I possibly could. I consulted my list as I held her hand, telling her of the news from home.

I had been talking to her for several minutes when I was interrupted by the bedside phone. I answered quickly so it wouldn't disturb Melissa, then realized how stupid that was—I would have put every phone in the world in here if there were even a small chance they would rouse her.

"Hello?"

"Hello, Marcus? This is Rob Johnson, from Jacksonville. Did I call at a bad time? Would you like me to call back later?"

Rob was a lawyer I had retained after the accident. While I didn't technically need a lawyer in Florida, I wanted someone to keep an eye on the case, to let me know what was going on.

I snorted. "I don't really know what a good time would be these days, Rob. Do you have any news?"

"None good, I'm afraid."

"What is it?"

"Coe's lawyer petitioned the court for a change of venue to New York, and they granted the petition."

"What?"

"I know. Listen, it might be different if you'd been here, but—"

"Listen, Rob. He committed the crime in Jacksonville, right? So how can they change the venue? How are the witnesses ever going to testify against him that far away?"

"They're not. That's the other news."

"I spoke with the District Attorney after the hearing, and he told me he had no choice but to accede to the venue petition—it was either that or drop the case completely. As it stands now, it probably won't even come to trial at all."

"How..." I was stunned.

"Listen a minute, okay?

"There were only three real witnesses that could help us."

"Right. The guy in the Volkswagen, the truck driver, and the Cadillac driver behind us. So?" I couldn't believe my ears.

"So they all backed out."

"What?"

"Faded away, didn't see a thing, left the area, whatever. They all changed their stories, and the most the DA could get without them was a DUI charge with minimal jail time, if any.

"Coincidentally enough, they all seem to have come into some money recently. The VW driver is driving a new Harley now."

"Rob, this can't be happening. If he bought them off, surely that itself would prove his guilt, wouldn't it?"

"If it could be proven he bought them off, yes, it would go a long way towards establishing his guilt. The DA says all the money seems to have come from aboveboard sources, new jobs, sales of property, that sort of thing, and he doesn't think an investigation would help—there are too many trails in too many states that will probably end up evaporating as soon as Coe's people find we've discovered the trails exist at all.

"Our best witness is in California right now, working for three times what he made here, working for a company Coe has ties to—but unless we can prove Coe ordered the job as a bribe, we can't do a thing. As far as the witness is concerned now, he can't remember anything to show Coe caused the accident."

The drunk's name was Andrew Coe, the principal in a variety of companies—a very rich man as well as being spoiled and well-connected businessman with layers of attorneys. He had been vacationing on a sailing craft of his that had stopped near Jacksonville on its way south when he took time out of his travels to cause the accident, took time out to destroy my family. As far as I could tell, he had become bored with the Intracoastal Waterway and had come into town, drunk, angry he could only find a Ford to rent. There was no clue as to why he picked us to chase. Of course, he wouldn't even admit he had done it at all, much less tell us why.

He had also been injured in the wreck, and had been granted permission to be flown back to New York for emergency treatment. His personal physician had raised holy hell to put him in "proper facilities," and threatened huge lawsuits against the state if Coe died while in Florida. He had a heart condition, true, but nothing that seemed medically out of the ordinary.

Coe's lawyer had assured the court that Coe would return, and he had been released on a bond of two hundred fifty thousand dollars, leaving the state immediately.

Until now I had no doubts he would be convicted. I knew he had money—that's why I had gotten so involved, to make sure his money wouldn't buy him out of this situation. I had been closely involved with the hearings, kept tabs on the witnesses, even paid for research when I thought it would help—I wanted to get this guy off the street for just as long as possible.

I had my girls moved back here as soon as they could be transported. I thought perhaps home surroundings would help, especially in Melissa's case. If I could only get her to see her other babies I hoped she would be okay.

I had gotten her this close, and she was stuck here. I couldn't let the other children see her often while she was this way, especially not while there was a chance she would have one of her fits. If she stayed this way much longer I would have to involve them more in her condition, to get them used to the idea she might never come home. I made sure they all visited Sam, especially before each operation, each invasion into her delicate little head. It was so hard. I hurt so much.

I hadn't realized that by leaving Florida I would hurt the case, but we had evidently taken the emotional pressure off the court by coming home. Since both Coe and my family were all legal residents of other states the courts had been glad to drop my hot potato as soon as they had an excuse. Coe was very rich and knew many influential people, and I could imagine elected officials felt a lot of pressure to pay as little attention to his case as possible. Florida is especially vulnerable in this regard since they elect their judges—an odd practice, to say the least.

"All right, Rob, I think I understand what's going on there. We seem to have lost for now. "Don't give up, though, because I want this guy in court."

Rob was confused. "I don't see how..."

"It ain't over 'til it's over, and that indictment is the closest we can come to hurting him. Even if the DA doesn't want to carry through with the criminal case, we'll sue his ass any way we can. He has to be punished! Has to!

"Here's what you do. I want to hire investigators for the witnesses, to see if we can find out anything about the bribes—especially the one in California—and I want to hire investigators for an even deeper look into Coe's background—New York, London, Timbuktu, wherever—I don't care. Okay?"

"Marcus, I'll do what I can, but you know you're probably flogging a dead horse—we'll never get this guy in court."

"We have to try, and I don't care which court or where. I'm going to hire a firm here in Lexington to coordinate things, so send me copies of the research we've done so far, now, today, and make sure I'm up on anything new. And don't let up down there—we're going to get this guy! If we can prove even one bribe it should be enough to infer guilt in other cases."

"All right, you're paying the bills. We're supposed to have a report on him from New York today, so I'll send that along as well—you should have it all tomorrow. Be careful with it, though—I won't have time to even look at it if you want it that fast."

"Listen, Marcus... don't do anything stupid, okay?"

"Thanks, Rob. We'll build this thing brick by brick until he's walled in—don't worry."

*I sat mesmerized by the burning circle fire in my dreams, watching the flames as intently as I did when I was awake.*

*Entering a meditative state, I knew somehow I was in a dream yet still felt the harmony of my inner self as a real thing, something sorely missed over the recent past.*

*Deep in this state I saw images begin to form, gradually becoming as real as they could be.*

*I found myself in a large twelve-sided chamber. A magnificent room without decoration or furniture, there was a simple wide-open arch in every wall with a different view through each.*

*Everything in the chamber was a luminescent white, glowing and mystical—the stucco walls, the expertly tiled floor, the high pearlescent dome above me—but it was the tableau outside the chamber that was fascinating. Each door led to a different place, as if to tell me there were many possible futures for me.*

*This chamber was not a destination, I knew, but a gateway, and I had to decide which of these arches to pass though. I don't know how I knew, but I didn't think I would be able to change my mind once I made my decision.*

*The true test of my self would be decided by my choice here.*

It was an hour drive to the medical center, so I couldn't get back and forth quickly. I decided to visit as usual in the morning but to come home early after checking on my patients to make sure the package had arrived from Jacksonville—I was going to get personally involved now.

Later, when I got home from the hospital, I spent a few minutes saying hello to everyone, including the kids just home from school, then went into our office-den to find two boxes full of files from Rob. I knew this had been a lot of work for him, and I hoped it would be worth it. No little file folder, this, but a box holding hundreds of papers, from exhibits to investigative reports to transcripts. I leafed through them for a few minutes, then decided to spread out a bit. Coe deserved to be punished for what he had done and I wasn't about to let him just drift away, no matter how much money he had, no matter who was in his pocket.

I had left Melissa's desk alone since the crash, carefully dusting it myself, but now I decided to use it for these files, to make it my command center. I felt it was important to leave my office as it was for any normal work I might be able to accomplish, but more importantly I wanted a place that was dedicated solely to this new research. I took a digital image of the top of her desk before I began, a reference for me so I could replace everything perfectly before she got home. I always hoped she would sit here again, and when she returned I wanted everything to be just as she had left it.

She would have wanted me to take care of the children before anything else, but they were in good hands and I was driven—I had to see this through. One of the casualties we had suffered was their innocence, and it hurt me to see how grown up their eyes were now, another price Coe had to pay.

I carefully removed everything from her desktop, placing each stack of papers and office accessory in an empty book box. When the large four-by-eight foot desk was clear of the clutter, I wiped it clean, then started her Macintosh.

I started a spreadsheet program to catalog everything, starting with the older files that I already had, making subject-related stacks, writing notes and reference numbers on each folder after I re-familiarized myself with the contents, then transferring the information to the computer. At some point in the reading and sorting I turned on the desk lamp.

I abandoned the spreadsheet for a relational database so I could include more complete information. Most people seemed to think all they needed to do was to buy a computer to organize their lives or jobs, not realizing all the effort it took to logically organize all their information. This was something I was used to doing—I wasn't as good as my Missy, but I could certainly hold my own.

When creating a database the starting point was an understanding for the type of information that might be needed later and a design that yielded information in an easy-to-understand format. Since the presentation of information was so often visual I did quite well at database construction, not satisfied until my end reports were simple, elegant, and understandable.

My stacks were beginning to be unruly, so I went to the supply cabinet in the office, noticing everyone had gone home for the day, then returning with several expanded hanging file pockets and two large metal hanging file frames to support them. Now I could be more methodical as I sorted the files, making even better notes as I became an expert on the subject of Andrew Coe and his visit to my home town.

I sorted and categorized until the original files were done, then went to the kitchen and made some coffee, pacing back and forth until it finished brewing, stretching and twisting to unkink my back. Fixing a cup and placing the rest in a thermal carafe, I went back to the den through the quiet house—I hadn't realized it was so late.

It was time to start on the newest box, the ones Rob had just sent. I knew I should sleep for a while, but I had to understand what I had and didn't have, and I knew there would be duplicates with some material already on hand. I couldn't sleep now—coffee would have to suffice. I wanted a whole picture in my mind before I rested, but knew it would take some time. I wanted to be able to see this man's life, to have an image I could rotate, manipulate, absorb, and understand.

There were more medical reports, reports on Coe's education, vacation spots, friends, family, and associates. I made an organizational chart in a superb new piece of 3D project management software, modifying it with each new piece of information, making a chart that looked like a three-dimensional family tree, growing larger and larger with each verified fact.

I would do the same thing when I got new information on the witnesses that had bailed on me—I thought they were my best hope of eventually convicting Coe.

As the false dawn showed itself in the night sky, I gave up for the night. After a nap I again visited the hospital with notes that I would keep nearby, updating them with thoughts throughout the day.

Every night now I would work on the files, restricting myself to three hours after the kids were asleep—even with this restriction my progress was swift. I connected the database and project management files so the database information was cross-referenced to the chart. This would allow me to get more detailed information by just double-clicking on any one of the three-dimensional "leaves" on the chart tree.

I finally came to the last file, very late in the evening after an intense week. In it there was an investigator's report of an accident Coe had caused in 1986, an accident that had caused the death of three people. I was amazed! Here was a report that showed he had done this before, actually killing his victims, destroying other families.

There was no paperwork on the outcome of the case, but the investigator indicated he would continue his research. Maybe I had something now, sure the court would have to punish a repeat offender.

Working deep into the early morning, I gathered the papers that showed a direction for continued investigation and faxed them to Rob's law office with a letter of explanation, so it would all be waiting for him when he got to his office. I instructed him to continue, searching through the records to find just how many times this maniac had gotten away with his crimes. I wanted every day of this man's life examined, every action scrutinized.

As he used his money and influence to escape punishment, I wanted to use mine to put him away. His life was shielded by lawyers and money, and I wanted to penetrate his defense.

I added a new type of label to the chart that highlighted these victims as well as my family—their names, date, location, and particulars—anything that appeared as though it was a crime flashed in orange now, to highlight his offenses. I added my family's information to the chart in glowing, impersonal orange.

I was creating a visual rendering of this man's life—he was my quarry now, and I would learn him the way I learned any prey. I would know more about him than his own mother, and I would stalk him and wait—wait with a reptilian patience, watch his every move.

I printed the files, flattening the chart by subject, and put them in a notebook for quick reference—this book would be my constant companion from now on, replacing the book where I kept my artistic ideas. I had put all of them on hold, for this was my creative endeavor now.

I was a hunter now, studying my quarry.

Shower time now, I went upstairs to get ready for another day at the hospital—I could take short naps there, and I needed to be with Melissa and Samantha.

I had never appreciated my own fame before, but it not only got me on all the news and talk shows, it almost forced me to speak out on our case—once the news of the personal disaster got out, everyone seemed to want an interview. I never realized so many people knew about me and about my work, both in art and archery. I grabbed the chance mightily, especially after the court case in New York had been dropped for lack of evidence—something we had expected by the time it happened. I took the time for these interviews to make sure he would be punished for something that he had done, at least one of the atrocities he had committed.

The media attention brought other facts to light. It turned out that Coe had hurt several people in his life of drunkenness and had bought his way out of every mess. A more complete picture was forming now, an image of arrogance.

My media campaign had little effect on Coe. He was not really a public figure and there was no real way to bring pressure to bear on him—sometimes he seemed like a ghost. I had seriously tried to use print, radio, and television to turn public opinion against him, but he seemed not to care except to keep even more out of public sight.

Our story was a sort of seven-day-wonder, but fizzled when it became obvious nothing was going to happen. We had uncovered three more crimes he had committed, but they were all closed cases, never to be opened again. A certain amount of notoriety had been attached to Coe's name, but that was all.

Oddly enough, the largest effect seemed to be on the sales of my catalog items, especially the arrows—the new demand was astounding. I didn't want to deal with training new employees, so I made the Business Manager take backorders and authorize overtime for that department, as long as the quality level could be maintained. I had samples from each batch delivered to me in my office, and I would sometimes study them—a growing pile of things I used to love, that used to matter to me.

I still practiced my archery, of course, but I couldn't seem to regain my center through its repetition. I had no choice but to shoot, for shooting a bow was as necessary to me as breathing, and it did help a little.

I had Coe's schedule now. Mr. Andrew P. Coe III could not stay anywhere without servants, without having homes opened and staffed, and once those staff members were known, so were his plans. An investigator of mine had confirmed what places he would stay through August and that he would retreat to Europe then for the foreseeable future, hoping, perhaps, that the publicity would die completely. I knew now he might be out of my reach for a year or more.

The only time he was scheduled to be in the eastern United States was July, at a vacation home in the Finger Lake region of New York state.

I had a new sense of urgency, desperate to get to him somehow before he left the country. It was inconceivable to me that he should escape, even without a current court case, and I couldn't let him go now. All my years of training in patience and meditation abandoned me in my need to bring this thing to justice.

I modified the database and chart, concentrated on every nuance of it until I knew his history well. I studied the investigators' reports and photographs, the layout of his New York house and grounds, the staffers and lackeys he would use, and the videotapes taken of Coe himself, both for the courts and news reports, as well as the surreptitious tapes taken by my investigators. I now knew his every habit pattern and preference as well as I knew my yado kata, and was merging my knowledge of him with a desire for revenge that only grew stronger as my knowledge increased.

I decided to keep this new information to myself until I might have some productive way to use it—I had enough information now. I called in all the investigators, dropped all lines of inquiry, and settled in to see what would happen next. I move all the boxed files to the basement and restored Missy's desk, only keeping my notebook in the den. I was figuratively hiding in my tree stand, waiting for him to walk underneath me, beginning to understand the difference between hunting a game animal and stalking a predator.

*I hung the dual portrait of Jessie and Sam in Jessie's office where I couldn't help but see it every day and night.*

*It had been created with all the love of a dedicated husband and father, a love that glowed as a pure, warm light, but now another aspect of that light showed—a darker, colder light that stood between the threat and threatened, devoid of pity or mercy.*

*An attack on those I loved struck much deeper than if it were aimed only at me.*

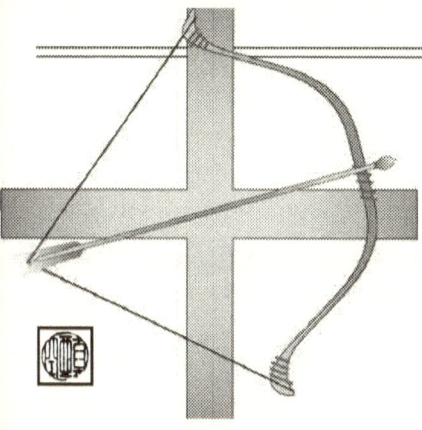

*1997*

# Kentucky-Pennsylvania

*Dreaming again, I reverently practiced the eight steps of kyudo with a concentration now unavailable to my waking self.*

*I could perfectly feel the Sanmi Ittai—the merging of mind, body, and bow—a unity that was always taught to practitioners, though rarely felt by most. Each stage of shooting merged with the next until I came in to kai, full draw, holding for several seconds while the energy concentrated.*

*The usual translation of kai is meeting, a time when all the elements have come together, each move taken with purpose to arrange for the next. It's not only a time for concentration and effort, but also for savoring each moment as the cumulative elements of a well-prepared shot build and exist together.*

*I became full and released sharply yet smoothly, I felt the instantaneous expansion and harmony that flowed from within me like reverberative waves of sound.*

*After the shot is taken the archer remains momentarily in position for this zanshin, remaining spirit or mind. The quality of zanshin is determined by the purity of kai and hanare (release), each stage of the shooting process building on the next.*

*It's important in zanshin to savor the seemingly brief instant that all our carefully prepared parts are together.*

Sam died in May, died in the middle of yet another delicate brain operation, died while we were separated from her by the rules that sequestered us in the waiting room, seemingly miles away. The children and Grandmother Rebecca were with me in the waiting room, pulled from their daily routine to be with us this dark and early morning.

Her spirit left her little broken body then, leaving us forever behind with our grief. We cried for her, me holding her over the protestations of the staff when they brought her out. She was surrounded closely by those awake and closest to her in all the world, and we didn't want to say goodbye. I rocked her little body back and forth as I sobbed, all of us holding onto one another. I racked myself until they pried me from her, ripping her innocent self away. My world ended there, never to be the same—I wanted to join her, to hold her forever.

I watched with my other babies as her small little sheet-covered body was wheeled away from us, stared after her as she left. We moved to Melissa's room, crying and wanting to be together. We didn't tell the unawake Melissa of Sam's death, but tried to include her in our grief, even though the sight of her lying there so still added to our hurt.

As a parent I had always known there couldn't be anything worse than having a child die before me, but the reality was so much worse than I had ever imagined that I couldn't stand it, even with the four and a half months of coma to prepare me. I forgot about Coe for the moment, the cause of all my grief.

All I knew was that my aloneness was complete now.

I was spent. After my family left I returned to Sam's room and, even though a nurse offered to do it for me, I removed all the drawings from the hospital wall myself, packing them neatly in a box. I knew it was one of my final duties to savor each artifact, each remembrance of my little girl's too-short visit with me on Earth. I carried the carton to Melissa's room and sat there for hours, not knowing what to say to her. The nurses gave us space.

I finally told Melissa, told her while I held her limp hand. I wasn't sure she knew what I was saying, but I thought I might have felt the pressure of her hand as she squeezed it a tiny bit. The thought of that squeeze heartened me, imagined or not, and it was a while before I left her side, crying with her over our loss. It wasn't just that my wife's skills complemented my own to make me whole, it was that I needed my mate to share my grief—she should be holding me and crying with me while I held her tightly in my grasp.

After what would have been suppertime for the conscious patients, I went home to be with everyone else. It wasn't easy to leave, but we needed to hold each other more, to mourn our poor little Samantha.

I hadn't realized how much everyone had allowed me my own room for grief over the past months, but my family clung so tightly to me now that I couldn't help but understand how alone we all were, those of us who were left alive and well.

The next few days were a blur. I finally decided to bury Sam in the town cemetery, as much as the thought of leaving her alone in the ground near only strangers was heartbreaking. Even though my own roots were spread far and wide in many places over the earth, the children thought of this as home, and to bury her anywhere else was unthinkable to them. I purchased enough plots so there would be room for more than all of us, leaving enough room for future decisions. Like most, I hadn't thought I would have to do this, somehow putting the decision far away into the future instead of accepting the possibility of losing someone close.

When I buried her I wrapped my gold equidistant cross and twenty-four inch chain around her arm to protect her when I was away, forever separated by six feet of hard-packed dirt. I had always thought that I would wish cremation for myself, but couldn't bring myself to do that to Sam, to further damage my little girl—it just seemed too final a step to take, even now—I didn't have the strength.

This burial made this little town in Kentucky my home now, no matter what I had thought before, gave me a tie I would never be able to deny again. I planted an oak tree on the corner double plot to make shade for my baby, and had a stone pew placed next to it so I could sit and talk to her in the days, weeks, and years to come. Perhaps one day I would carve a bench of my own to replace it. Unbidden, an image came to me of the bench, Sam's little face on the front of one arm, the other end spreading into a large chunk of raw rock to indicate the unfinished nature of her little life.

It was fortunate that the business could run without me, for the most part. It was also fortunate that I didn't need to create many new pieces of art, for my world had dimmed—colors went unnoticed, sounds unheard, life unlived. My world contracted into a dense and dark little ball, with room only for my family, wife, and training—nothing else mattered.

As with any business, I had long-term relationships with those who were special to me, such as Kimiko-chan, my old language teacher from Japan. She had blossomed in her relationship with me and had for years run a small gallery in Kyoto with her husband. In a very real sense her success depended on people like me to supply her with a constant flow of art, and that flow from me had been interrupted. She shared my heartache, of course, but part of me still felt guilty for abandoning her.

There were others like her, people who called me directly instead of the office manager, and I owed these people a great deal, though I didn't have it in me to help them now.

My life was split between home and the hospital, where I now concentrated solely on Melissa's needs. There had to be a way to bring my darling back.

At the hospital, I finally was able to make the doctors be honest with me, and their news wasn't good—not many came out of a coma that lasted this long, no matter what the cause. I became even more determined not to lose her as I had our little girl—I read to her more, talked to her more, told her our own old stories all over again, secretly seething inside for our loss.

There were small signs of improvement. The little squeeze I felt the day Sam died was not something I imagined, but the first of many little squeezes. The doctors didn't believe me at first, but eventually had no choice, for one day a tear rolled down her cheek as she squeezed my hand. It was almost as if our daughter's death had allowed her to start facing things, to take a tentative step back into life. Some part of her had heard me.

Two weeks after Sam died, the witness in California died as well, died with a bullet in his brain. I had Rob, my lawyer, check on the circumstances but he couldn't tell me anything concrete. It looked like a random shooting, but this had been the only witness that had ever wavered in his loyalty to Coe, and I felt like the coincidence was just too much. We had slowed our investigation for want of progress, but Rob and I knew we would eventually have been able to prove Coe's complicity in bribery if we had continued the search. After Sam's death there had been renewed interest, both legally and in the media, since any new charge would have now been more serious, and perhaps Coe was feeling renewed pressure no matter how many judges and politicians he controlled with his money and influence. At any rate, this death brought Coe fully to my attention.

If Coe had in fact had anything to do with the death, then I felt there was a good chance either Missy or I were next on his list. I was seemingly the only person who had ever refused to buckle under his pressure and was fast becoming a thorn in his side. I felt he would sense that he was more secure if we were out of the way. Perhaps I was paranoid, but I wasn't about to give him a chance now—I made my decision, a decision for revenge made from the perspective of my now-contracted world. I was convinced that any attack I made would be defensive, no matter how savage or final.

While I spent time with Missy every day, I planned revenge on Coe every night.

If I had been honest with myself I might have been able to admit that I wasn't completely sure just how real Coe's threat was, for it was possible that I wanted him to be a threat just to provide an outlet for my renewed anger. His very existence now was like the misdirection of a magician, and I gladly looked there, unwilling to be objective in my assessment.

Something Rob said had stuck in my head—Coe had been difficult to convict because "there were too many trails in too many states." It made me think, and once thinking, to plan. My plot against Coe automatically became another creative challenge for me, its morality hidden by the familiar problem-solving process.

I studied my files concerning the New York hideaway I knew Coe owned on Skaneateles Lake, along with photos I had of the house and surrounding area. It was only one of his hideaways, one of his many ways to escape, and a place where I knew he was scheduled to stay in July. His movement from one home to another normally protected him from public view and protected him, but it now would give me a chance to find him relatively unprotected.

I studied topo maps and road maps of the area, as well as larger maps, gradually formulating a plan that should work, getting rid of Coe while leaving me undiscovered. I don't think I would ever have considered this plan if I thought I would be caught—I still needed to take care of my family, and his life wasn't worth the loss of mine. I made a list of the things I would need, spending many creative days to make sure I had considered all the possibilities. Planning something like this was new to me, and I tried to consider everything that might go wrong.

Without telling anyone, I bought a used car one morning in Lexington, a 1991 Honda CRXsi, a sporty little black thing that would do one twenty-five an hour if asked. I was careful not to touch the inside very much when I bought it, and wiped the places clean where I had touched it after I left the dealership. I had worn a hooded sweatshirt with my hair tucked into it, a crushed hat, and plain glasses that I didn't need. I liked the outfit—it seemed to take just the edge off of my all-too-recognizable appearance. I picked up similar clothes for my trip, but darker, a collection of clothes that made me appear completely unremarkable.

I had paid cash for the CRX and gotten away without having to use any ID, counting on the salesman's greed. I had told him that I had forgotten my wallet, but he had sold me the car anyway, knowing I would have to use my ID when I registered it, something I never intended to do.

Knowing that the game plan was complete, I drove the car to Charleston, West Virginia, one morning, careful to obey the speed limit, then parked it in the long-term lot at the airport. It had been a careful three-hour drive to Charleston, and even with the bus ride home I was back at the hospital before dark.

I told Rebecca I was going to a shoot in Michigan, and she was delighted. She had been worried about my brooding, and thought that I needed a break. I loaded the RV with my normal complement of gear, the cell phone, and the new set of supplies, leaving a few days later, back to Charleston.

I carefully traded vehicles at the airport lot, taking the prepared duffle bag and encased bow from the RV to the CRX. I drove straight up I-79 to I-90, pushing to make it to the Syracuse area during the deepest part of night. I slept in the car at a rest stop, then spent two days and nights scouting the Auburn and Skaneateles Lake area, taking notes on the house and environment.

I showered at truck stops and ate from food I had brought with me, always wearing one of the two matching outfits I had brought. These black jeans and dark-blue hooded sweatshirts hid my normal appearance, which I think worked quite well. The hood bunched up at the back of my neck, hiding the braid running down my back inside the shirt, and the unneeded glasses helped as well, changing my face. My dark crush hat completed the transformation, hiding the fact I had long hair. No one would have been able to recognize me from what I thought were my most distinctive features, and these clothes were a type I had never really worn before, down to the dark sneakers purchased especially for this trip.

Parking well after dark at an unused residence near Coe's I had researched, I carefully and quietly worked my way to his house, also uninhabited now. Fighting the knowledge and fear of my invasion into another person's property, I studied the house closely from the shrubbery surrounding the yard, actually sneaking up to the house under cover of darkness to look in the windows and fix the front door's position into the GPS receiver/plotter. It would show me a backlit map of the exact spots I had marked, as well as how far I was from each point. This hand-held electronic marvel used the satellites in the Global Positioning System to fix locations in its memory, to a maximum of two hundred if I needed them, ten points on twenty routes, and his front door would be fixed as the terminus of route one. I next used it to mark hiding places that allowed me to watch the house. I noted the cars here, noted them carefully, not knowing whether they belonged to Coe or his staff. Leaving the area, I entered points on my route while I drove, ending the last point of my route with the entrance to I-81.

Until I erased it, this device would always be able to recall these positions, no matter how far away I was, no matter how dark the night or fierce the weather.

Satisfied with my research here, I marked my route on a throwaway map, I-81 down to 13 to 17, then west to Olean and down 446 and 6 to the barn close to Denton Hill. I wanted an uncrowded route for my plan, a plan that would use the annual shoot here in a few weeks. I drove the route, noting times at each major road change, marking this as route two in the GPS reader. Four hours to the barn, near enough. I got there around midday with a recently-filled tank of gasoline.

I stopped on highway 6 near the barn, watching to see if the traffic was as sparse as I remembered. Satisfied, I pulled the car in the hard-packed drive far enough off the road to hide it from passersby, marking this as the last point of route two.

I got out, walking softly, and made sure the barn was as hidden and deserted as I remembered. Looking through the cracks I saw that the inside was still dust-covered and deserted.

I opened the wide door, drove in and parked, then closed the door again from the outside, obliterating any tire tracks while outside. I marked the location with the GPS device as the start of route three, then started walking through the woods toward the Denton Hill site, deserted this time of year. I took a small survival kit, my electronic mapping gadget, and archery equipment, including two yado shafts—I didn't expect to run into a new pack of dogs this time, but certainly wasn't going to go through here unprepared.

The fight I had with the dogs had burned this terrain into my brain, and I had no trouble following my old path, marking each turn on my hand-held device, keeping notes in the margin of the large road map. When I reached the end of the field where I had parked five years ago I crouched and watched for awhile, noting exactly where I wanted to park the RV. I then retraced my wooded path, the passage I would take under cover of darkness in July, a path I would have to take without the device.

When I got back to the barn I took a nap in the car, leaning the seat all the way back. I awakened before dark and packed things up, leaving most of my gear, archery equipment included, in the car. I wrapped the GPS device and map in a plastic bag and buried them in the soft, fine dirt in a corner. The lithium batteries would store my three routes for ten years or more, their incriminating access protected by a required password.

Incriminating. It was the first time I used the word, even to myself, and it stopped me.

As I stood in the deserted structure and contemplated the tools I had assembled, the magnitude of my scheme struck me. Perhaps it was knowing that everything was in place now to commit murder, perhaps it was actually performing reconnaissance on Coe's house, perhaps it was even the physical proximity and the memory of the only life-or-death encounter that had ever required my training—something triggered my higher self to look at what I was planning.

Was this something I could do? Was this something I should do? Was this something I had the right to do? Was there a choice? Why hadn't this bothered me before?

It was true I had been trained over many years in a martial art, an art designed to defeat another. It was also true that I had used that art in self defense, even to the death, even against multiple opponents. Being prepared was one thing, though, and planning in advance something altogether different—one was almost instinctive while the other carried the seeds of evil.

Didn't it?

I sat in the car and closed my eyes, trying to visualize events. I saw Coe as I knew him and imagined him standing in front of me, face-to-face.

Did I consider him an animalistic creature—like the dogs—or was he human to me? Would I be able to attack in coldest blood if he didn't initiate an attack? Even if he did, would I hold back? I had never even been in a serious fight, even in childhood.

Not only had I never been in a fight, I had never been in trouble. I grew up in a neighborhood where, as in most, my family and neighbors were law-abiding citizens—I didn't even vaguely remember an encounter with the police, though I remembered the apprehension of that confrontation if I even contemplated breaking the law. The fear of being exposed in front of my family, friends, and neighbors was a powerful force, a negative force that kept me on the straight and narrow, a force complemented nicely by the positive values my parents and teachers gave. I had known people in high school who had a reputation for stealing things or selling drugs, but I was never attracted to their company. I never participated much in the drug culture—it always seemed to me that the people selling drugs were not the type you could trust. Trust. Perhaps that was the answer.

If you counted someone as a friend you trusted them, and even if they were only an acquaintance you assumed a faith they would be a positive and supporting influence, didn't you? I had always assumed that those around me could be trusted at some level, and didn't they also have the right to expect that they could trust me the same way? Didn't that include a basic faith that you would not harm another?

I tried to imagine how my view of my friends would change if I knew they had killed someone. It was difficult at first, but it didn't take long to see what would make such an act palatable—defense. Only if someone were directly attacked without any other recourse could an act of violence be justified, and even then it was a stretch. Perhaps it was a strictly American viewpoint, something I remembered that was called the "Popeye syndrome"—an act of violence was only justifiable after an unprovoked attack. Anything else was cowardly and wrong.

Somehow Coe was able to turn off this sense of responsibility, but could I? No matter how deeply I felt theoretically threatened by this man or how many others he might destroy in the future, could I intentionally harm him when his threat was only hypothetical? Wasn't I instigating an attack myself by going to his home?

What if I was right in my judgement that he was going to harm either Melissa or me? Did that really change things?

Was there an alternative? Better security, perhaps, or moving my family to another state or country?  Wouldn't running away be safer and more justifiable, even if it were cowardly at some level?  What price would I pay to commit murder, and would my internal anguish be worse than prison—or death?  Would I be able to look my little ones in the eye if I committed this act?

As I searched for an answer, I tried to visualize a discussion with Coe, an attempt to find an answer, and I realized another flaw in my plan: He was never alone.  Many of those who sought wealth and power seemed to surround themselves with others hungry for the same things—lawyers, business associates, nephews, children, sons-in-law—anyone who smelled easy money and would not let ethics stand in their way.  Only Coe's opinion would count to these people, and they would break almost any law to curry favor with him.  He was always with several of these sycophants, and I didn't know how many traveled with him.  I realized this was a different issue, though, and set it aside for now.

I finally decided to leave things in place here while seriously searching for an alternative.  If I found a better answer I would simply remove these things from the barn later, something I was sure I wouldn't regret even after all my work.  As I prepared to leave I rechecked everything—I knew that the barn wasn't secure and the car was at risk, but a part of me wouldn't be upset if the car would be missing when I returned.  I was taking a chance, leaving the car here, but felt I had to take the risk.

The recurve bow I had chosen was as inconspicuous as I could find.  It was sixty inches long when strung and had a draw weight of fifty-five pounds, plenty for my needs.  This was a current factory production bow, so I could dispose of it when I had to, if I thought it was necessary, without risking that it would be traced back to me.  I had chosen to use my own arrows, but from the business stock, not my personal collection.  The arrows I used could be considered my signature, the obvious clue leading directly back to me, so I had to be careful—at least as careful as I had been with fingerprints.

I covered the car with an old clear plastic tarp, cracked and discolored until it was the color of the dirt floor.  I checked to make sure that the barn looked untouched from the outside, then settled down with my small backpack to wait.

At full dark I walked west on the side of the road, hiding whenever a car passed.  Literally sneaking through Coudersport I kept walking most of the night until I reached a small town named Smethport.

In Smethport I purchased a bus ticket for Pittsburgh, then slept after I boarded the bus. Once I reached the city I bought another ticket to Charleston, then ate lunch in a crowded diner. Once on the bus in a back seat I started a list of potential alternatives to my situation, and knew that I would make a very serious effort to make an alternative plan. In Charleston I took a local bus to the airport and retrieved the RV, then headed towards home, stopping on the way to take a shower and change clothes. I washed and dried the now-dirty clothes at a suburban laundromat, then tucked them in a seldom-used storage area under a seat until I needed them again, wrapping the sneakers in a plastic bag.

I stopped at the hospital when I got to Lexington to check on Melissa, staying for awhile. I called Rebecca to tell her where I was and to let her know I would be home after supper. She was close to panic—she had tried to get me on the cell phone and couldn't. I kicked myself for not thinking of that, having left it turned off in the RV, then explained it by telling her I had been out of range. I knew now that unexplainably being out of touch was a flaw in the plan I had made, something a professional would have probably seen right away.


*Melissa continued to improve, slowly, under everyone's daily care.*

*Not really aware of things around her yet, I was overjoyed just to see her move, even a little. I was certain she would hold me again, hug me one day all by herself.*

*Just knowing that I could turn away from my plan of murder further lightened my heart. Perhaps I would take her home after Denton Hill, if I could, to mend her.*

*When a practitioner loses the way it is important to return to the basics, something I had known for years in my kyudo study. I now applied the concept to my sumi-e, using the control gained through the years to make one practice painting after another in Melissa's room, a calming influence on both of us. As I had used the authority of my flow to create a expansion of myself over the years, now I used the skill that was deep in my bone and blood to begin to regain my self.*


I was trying to be rational about Coe and his situation as it related to me, trying to balance my desire for revenge with my family's safety. I had finally come to the conclusion that murder was not in me, that the only violence I could contemplate was in direct defense. There would have to be another answer.

As I worked out my situation my daily schedule fell into a very predictable routine, a routine that revolved around my family, and I had plenty of time to consider my options. I took security very seriously, hiring a firm to watch over my family—something I should have thought of earlier, and would have, if I had been thinking sensibly. I started carrying a tube with yado shafts in it wherever I went—a quiver of sorts, covered in vinyl with a shoulder strap an a zipper that would give me quick access. Coe's benign nature was not something I felt I could trust—he was still my enemy, and I knew that he felt the same about me. If he came to me in anger all my questions would answer themselves, for he would become as an attacking dog, something I could deal with easily. Of course, I realized that it would be more likely that he would hire someone else for the job, but the principle remained the same, I thought.

Missy was doing well, and seemed to care about the time I spent with her. I made sure there were others to stay with her when I had to be away, and the kids spent their own healing time with her. The signs of improvement were unmistakable now, small signs that meant everything to my family, and I felt it was safe to let them hope for her recovery, to re-bond. On the day that she briefly opened her eyes I knew that there was no room in my life for an enemy, that I needed to concentrate on healing. I had built my defense against my enemy, and didn't want to worry about him any longer.

I called Rob's law firm in Florida and left a message for him to return my call. When he did we spoke for a few minutes about how everyone was doing, especially Melissa—he had become my friend over the past months and was genuinely concerned about my family. I didn't tell him of my original plan, of course, but was honest about my current concerns about Coe. I asked Rob to speak with him directly, if possible, and to let him know that I was done, that the war was over. He assured me he understood and that he would get back to me. He seemed genuinely relieved that I had freed myself from a desire for revenge, for he had sensed the hate in me and had been worried. Another flaw.

I was still worried about what Coe might attempt to do to me or my loved ones in the future, to sanitize his record in the most permanent way, but I had to let it go. I was needed here.

Day after day I continued to work with Melissa and to be with my family—they all needed me.

I still had to retrieve my gear from Pennsylvania and felt the archery trip would serve the added purpose of providing a break from my now-established yet tiring routine. My tentative plan was to arrive at Denton Hill late Monday afternoon, July twenty-first, a few days before the actual shoot began, but the timing wasn't critical any longer, and I could take my time.

Rebecca knew Denton Hill was important to me, and wanted me to go, even though I would be gone an entire week. I paid special attention to her concerns about the phones, since we had received literally thousands of calls from both well-wishers and cranks over the past few months, so I had a separate unlisted phone line installed in the kitchen under one of the business names. She made sure that family, close friends, the kid's schools, the medical center, and the doctors had the number, but was very tight about how many other people had it.

I told her I would call her with the phone number as soon as I got it, but that the office might not be staffed that early in the week, though there was also a pay phone on the outside lower level of the lodge. She was a little worried about me being out of touch, remembering that there was no cell coverage at Denton Hill, but things had been going so smoothly lately that she wasn't too upset.

*I held my sweetheart's hand in mine, saying good-bye to her before leaving for Pennsylvania. I told her I was going to the shoot, and I was knew she understood my need to get away.*

*My lady was soon to be thirty-nine years old, seven years my junior, but she was still my bride, and I would miss her.*

*I wanted to get it over with, to erase the evidence of my embarrassing lapse from sanity, to come back here to heal her, to start over again.*

As I drove by the barn near Denton Hill I craned my neck to look, but couldn't see well enough to tell if the area had been disturbed in the weeks since I had left the car. It had been nerve-racking to leave it there all this time, but I would know tomorrow if I had misjudged the situation—I knew barns like that could literally go for years without being disturbed and had tried not to worry about the tarp-covered vehicle.

The person who checked me in at the gate was not someone I knew, so I accepted my dated receipt and drove to the camping area.

I set up the RV in the same spot I had used in 1992, facing the door toward the large field instead of away as I had originally planned, the only vehicle in the remote camping area so far. This shoot had grown so large so fast that I knew I wouldn't be alone for long. Last year there had been over fifteen hundred people here—they had even had to turn some folks away—and I was guessing it would be even bigger this year, crowding a lot of people and vehicles together by the end of the week. I rolled out the awning, set out a couple of chairs with coolers, created a fire pit, and in general made everything quite "homey" and welcoming.

The start of any events weren't scheduled until Thursday, so until then there would just be old friends getting together, practicing on the three hillside courses and on the practice ranges. Things wouldn't get even a little busy until Wednesday afternoon.

No one here really knew I had arrived yet, I thought, and if they did they would probably visit me at the RV tonight. I thought that if no one showed, I probably wouldn't be missed after I left—I hoped. Officially I was here, and that's what counted. All I could do was cross my fingers and work to set everything straight.

Tonight would have been the night I would have left for New York, and I had counted on the presence of only a few campers in the beginning of the week.

I ate, then took a light nap until midnight, part of me listening for the knock I hoped wouldn't come. I got up, brushed my teeth, took a shower, then put on my regular clothes and gear, stuffing a folded thirty-gallon drawstring trash bag in my back pocket.

I took Kiko's Dog Bow and left the RV quietly. It would probably be four or five hours before I returned. I knew I would have no problem finding my way, even in the dark, but allowed for extra time—I wanted to get everything I had left in the barn and turn the CRX around so I could tow it away. I planned to leave the shoot late Sunday afternoon after most others had left, and it should be safe to get the car relatively unseen. After I somehow disposed of it everything would be safe again and my life could return to normal.

I saw well in the dark and it was only one night past the full moon, so I didn't expect to use my little flashlight—most people don't realize how visible they are when they use a light, that the light itself can be seen very far away. I remembered this path well now, and walked carefully over the small hills that were becoming familiar to me.

It was eerily beautiful walking here at this time, dappled shadows and pleasant temperatures. I walked over the lip of a small rise and beheld an almost circular hollow about twenty yards across, almost bare of vegetation. The moonlight showed through the trees, lighting the grayish and sandy earth like a place of worship. I watched, wondering why this spot seemed so special.

I decided to sit in the center for a time, to clear myself.

*I found myself again in the large twelve-sided chamber, but this time the location was no mystery—it was the bowl in the woods where I sat, the doors now paths leading in all directions over the artificial horizon so close all around me.*

*It was obvious to me now that I was at a spiritual crossroads, again at a place with many possible futures.*

*I had to decide which of these paths to walk. Coe was still deeply in my thoughts. Perhaps I needed to engage him somehow still, banish him once and for all to free my soul of the darkness he had imposed on me and mine.*

*What if I continued with my plan? Everything was still in place, still waiting under the dirt in the old barn.*

When I got to the barn I put my gear in a trash bag from the my small pack—including the Kiko bow and my clothes—then stuffed the bag quietly and gently under a bush outside. Only when it was hidden did I take my stalking clothes out of the little pack, covering my nakedness again. I wanted to cut any ties between Denton Hill and the little black car, to cross-contaminate as little as possible.

I didn't turn my flashlight on until I had opened the barn slowly, quietly. Noting several small clues I had been careful to place, I made sure that the tarp hadn't been touched, then dug up the hidden GPS device and map. I checked the gear I had left, including the Dream Catcher bow, warmed up the car when it (thankfully) started, then turned on the GPS device, marking myself at the start of route two. I backed out, closed the door and started my journey, carefully and quietly.

Dawn found me waiting in the bushes at Coe's house at Skaneateles Lake, the car hidden in the driveway of the neighboring unused house. I knew the house, knew that it would be empty, and had driven into the drive as if I had belonged there.

I waited patiently through the day, confident in my hiding place, seething when I saw Coe.

He came outside twice in the morning, once to swim, once to read a book in a hammock. I saw him cringe when he entered the cold water, and was tempted to transfix him in the hammock as he slept, but I stayed my hand, needing the dark to return safely from New York to Pennsylvania.

He left for the country club around two o'clock, and I settled down for another nap, careful not to disturb my surroundings, lying carefully on a thin camo tarp. It was well after dark when I awoke, jerking myself around to make sure that he hadn't returned yet, seeing immediately that his car was still gone.

I gathered everything into the pack except for my bow and quiver and readied myself for his return, eating some trail mix. I put on my skintight Damascus gloves and made sure everything was wiped clean. I waited until dark before I moved over to the side of the house.

Coe didn't return until after one a.m., much later than I had expected, missing the lighted driveway's edge as he tried to park. I had been waiting quietly in the shadows and didn't move until he had left the car and was coming up the concrete drive. I moved into the light, hands free, quiver on my back.

When he saw me he stopped, but didn't react right away, swaying a little.

When he realized who I was, his eyes grew large in disbelief. He reached in his jacket and pulled out a small .38 special revolver, waving it in my direction.

By the time he had the gun out I had two shafts in my hand, swinging them in the yado kata I had practiced for so many years, swinging the left one first in a graceful arc. I was using two of my target shafts with field points, the same shafts available for purchase through many different sources. The blued-steel point smashed against the tendons on the back of his right hand, paralyzing it with pain, forcing him to drop the gun.

At the same moment the shaft I held in my right hand kissed the left side of his neck near the front, opening his jugular vein, beginning to literally drain the life out of him. A bladed shaft would have made a cleaner cut, but I knew the skin over his neck was thin, the vein near the surface offering little resistance. I moved to the right as I swung, sidestepping the spray of blood as he crumpled off the side of the drive in the grass. He rolled over on his back, looking for the gun even as the blood drained from his body, flinging his left hand on the ground, palm up.

I took the shaft in my right hand and shoved it through his left, passing it between the bones deep into the ground even as I hit his Adam's apple with the other shaft, crushing his larynx, stopping any cry he might have let escape. As he tried to reach for the shaft sticking out of his impaled hand and for his throat simultaneously, he saw his blood for the first time. His eyes went wide again before they glazed over, not enough alcohol-laced blood left in him to sustain consciousness.

I moved his right hand back over to his side with the remaining shaft's tip, then stabbed it through as well, sticking him to the ground like the bug he was, a curious zoological specimen captured forever.

It was over. Months of hate and planning had culminated in a battle that had only lasted a few seconds.

As the river of blood slowed to a trickle I had my first chance to feel an emotion, any emotion. I had come here for a confrontation, true, but had forgotten how automatic my reactions were when I used yado. The severity of my actions were flamed, I suppose, by my hatred, an emotion I had never really felt for anyone before.

I expected to feel more, but I was emotionally drained. If it hadn't been for my family I would have gladly turned myself in, right here, right now, but now I had no choice but to complete my plan. I took off my left glove and felt gently for a pulse that couldn't exist, just to reassure myself that it was finally over, then wiped the area where I had touched in case a print could have been left.

I checked the scene to make sure I hadn't left any clues other than the obvious ones, the arrows standing up through his hands. I had used a design I called USA Arrows, shafts decorated with a bright blue back end, long bright red tip, white stripes and feathers. One of my most popular, I used them here for the sense of justice they brought to me.

I picked up my gear, checking again for clues, making sure I left no tracks as well as I could in the dark, then quietly made my way back to the car.

I didn't make it back to the barn until a half hour before light. I had stopped for gas the previous evening, so fuel wasn't an issue, and it was only my tiredness that worried me now—I wanted no mistakes.

I left everything in the car except for the bow and tackle, the map and the GPS device, using it to guide me back to camp after trading clothes. Nothing in the car should incriminate me now, except perhaps the shoes or gloves, but the car's existence itself would be the giveaway that I had to worry about. I had to be patient for now, just a few more days. I moved quickly but was full of purpose.

When I made it back to the RV I checked everything, noting it had rained lightly most of the night.

It was full light now, and I picked up the Olympus D-300L digital camera. I took it outside after setting up some bows and sets of arrows, then took a series of shots to prove I had been here this morning. I used standard resolution except for close-ups, using my photographer's eye to take several shots. When I was done I took everything back inside, downloaded the photos and wiped the internal six megabyte memory clean.

I called Rebecca, giving her the numbers I had promised. She sounded normal, as I hoped I did. I said hello to a few folks while I walked to the lodge and back.

I took a short nap, then a shower, giving myself some time to think and feel.

Coe was gone. I didn't expect to feel either relief or remorse, but what I hadn't expected was the feeling of shadow, of shame. Who was I to be capable of this thing?

After I dressed and made coffee I wandered about the camp taking a few photos with the digital camera, thinking about the new changes in my life, so different today than yesterday.

I knew that I would be the most likely suspect in Andrew Coe's death, but didn't know how quickly they could find me when they looked. If his death made the Kentucky news I knew I could expect a call from Rebecca, but not many people had the new unlisted number, so I didn't think it would be easy to track me here if his death didn't make the national news. It was my job now to act as normal as a grieving yet recovering parent and husband could, hiding my nervousness. Would I betray myself? Could I convincingly lie? The path I had chosen now was diametrically opposed to my own sense of who I was.

By the end of the day I had visited several people and their camps, commiserating on the lousy weather of the day before that had kept me inside, trading business cards with some new friends, accepting condolences of old friends and others that knew my situation. I had an interesting conversation about arrow weight and flight distance, and made sure that two or three people that I knew visited me at the RV, so they would know the way it was set up.

I dumped my paper map in a campfire as soon as the opportunity presented itself, stirring the remains until they were gone. The map burned quickly—I was sure that a few more days' ashes would hide all traces of the paper. It was kind of sad, really, all that work gone, but both these things had more than served their purpose.

I had wiped all locations out of the GPS receiver, but re-recorded new routes one, two, and three just to be sure, set new coordinates while visiting sites in a random fashion. Later that afternoon I re-wiped the routes, then took the battery out and reinstalled it, making sure it was empty before putting it under the driver's seat. Everything should have been clean now except for the car and its contents.

I had to take another nap, but was interrupted by a knock on the door about seven o'clock. It was a volunteer worker, leaving the message that I needed to call my mother-in-law. I thanked him, then brushed my teeth before going up to the lodge to call.

The police had called Rebecca looking for me, and had told her why—she was frantic. I told her not to worry and that I would be home as fast as I could. This seemed to be working out well. I was glad that I wouldn't have to stay all week and wanted to get back to the protection of my own home—and assuredly my own lawyers.

It was dark before I could get away, because I let a few key people know what was going on so they could pass the word. My news caused a lot of excitement—the news stories of a few months before had been a major source of conversation with everyone I had visited today. There weren't any tears shed for Andy Coe here, and I was sure that the method of his death would cause a lot of excitement when the news spread. The only news I had shared was the only news I had received from Rebecca, that he was dead, and I might be a suspect.

Several people made sure I had their names, so they could be witnesses that I had been here. I was sorry that I couldn't stay longer, because I wanted people to have fuzzy memories of the beginning of this week, to forget that they hadn't really seen me on Tuesday. Maybe I could fly back later in the week.

Highway six was deserted, as usual, and I turned left onto it until I reached the barn, then pulled off. I went to the barn and pulled the car out, putting the tarp in the back storage section. I checked the barn over under strong light, wiping any trace that a car had been there with some brush, then closed the old door.

I said a little prayer, then pulled the car up behind the RV in the proper position, then went back to wipe any remaining tracks. Moving the car was scary, but it had to be moved. I got out the tow bar, connecting it to the RV and the car, then pulled out, circling Coudersport on a small road that I had discovered the night I walked through town.

From here south it would be back roads, south by southwest to Pittsburgh. It took a few hours to get there, but once I did I left the CRX parked in a part of town that looked less-than-prosperous, counting on its theft. The streets were fairly deserted on this weeknight, but with the driver's window down and the keys in the ignition, I was sure the car would be gone soon. The tow bar was wiped off and back in its storage place, with no new marks on it that I could see.

From Pittsburgh I went to Columbus, stopping the RV next to a Salvation Army receptacle where I planned to leave the clothes I had worn, next planning to place the tarp and other miscellanea in several dumpsters around the city. After I'd gotten rid of all these things I would feel I was clear.

As I opened the door to the Salvation Army box I was startled by a spotlight and the red-white flash-flash-flash of a police cruiser behind the RV with a barked command to "freeze." My heart leapt to my throat.

*Startled, I found myself again in the woods near Denton Hill, the moon past its zenith, the air still clear. I was still not a murderer.*

*Perspective. I was still not a murderer. It was still not too late to erase the shadow I had been feeling in my reverie.*

*Even though I had the power and the skill to eliminate Coe, I knew now that his death at my hand would have changed my life irretrievably, making it worse than it was now—something I hadn't believed possible.*

When I saw the barn I felt a strong sense of déjà vu, like I was coming back here again and again, feeling especially eerie in the moonlit darkness. I opened the door carefully, then sensed that something was wrong. I closed the door and turned on the little flashlight, then saw that the tarp was still there, but the CRX was missing, only a dirt floor where the car had been.

I quickly turned off the light, my heart pounding. As I stood there I tried to speculate about what might have happened and what I should do next—the only thing I could imagine was that the car had been discovered and taken, perhaps by the barn's owner, perhaps by someone else.

I had considered this possibility often, yet didn't know whether I should be worried or relieved. Whoever took the car and its contents had really done me a favor, but it denied me the opportunity to erase the literal tracks I had left in the previous weeks, and that bothered me.

Finally gathering my wits I turned the flashlight back on and checked the place where I had buried the GPS device, thankfully finding it and the map there. Confused, I looked both inside and outside the barn for any possible clues to the car's disappearance, turning out the light again when none could be found.

The only illegal thing I had done was to not register the CRX, but that didn't stop the fear that gripped me.

*It was something I had learned from competition with a compound bow.*

*In the beginning of training an archer is overjoyed just to hit the target. Joy leads to further practice and the process of discovery that teaches, first the mechanics that need adjustment, then the techniques that settle. As more shots tend to enter the circles closer to the center, the score per game rises, and each additional point gained in the overall average gains in importance, always counting up.*

*Gradually the point total per game rises from the "B" class point range into the "A" class and then slowly into the very highest ranks of "AA." The joy changes to a sense of confidence, knowing that each and every shot is heading for the five ring.*

*Once firmly in AA the process begins again, the smaller "X" ring now the only important part of the target.*

*At this stage of training, the archer stops counting up and only sees the misses, deductions from the ever-important X count, arrow placement that counts in fractions of an inch, sometimes very small fractions.*

*Before the accident I had measured my professional and family life as would a champion score a game, concerned only with tiny deductions from perfection. Since that day, though, I was again a beginner, trying to count any points I could find to increase my average.*

*In this sense I had counted the decision not to confront Coe as a great step forward. I knew I would have a lot of work to rebuild all that I held dear, but that it was not only possible but necessary.*

*My worst fear now was that my intentions would be discovered, that the temporary fall into darkness would be revealed to those that held me dear.*

Back in the RV I tried to consider the possibilities. I had to try to imagine the risks in light of all the evidence someone now held.

By the next day I had decided that there were but three possibilities: If everything had been taken by a simple thief—even if that thief was the owner of the barn—I was probably fairly safe, I thought, because anything of value would be sold and the rest thrown away; if, somehow, the police had somehow been informed of the unlawful storage of the car then it all might be in their possession, the situation would be very different, and dangerous; the third possibility, the most remote, was that Coe somehow discovered my plans and took the car and equipment himself.

At first the likelihood that Coe was involved had seemed remote, but then I realized that he was the very person who had the resources to keep me under surveillance, and the only person who would benefit from my misfortune. If I had been confronted with the evidence that connected me to Coe, what would I be able to say? "Oh, well, yes, I actually had planned to kill him, but changed my mind...?" Even I wouldn't believe that.

While shooting at the Denton Hill practice range with new arrivals Monday afternoon I had the thought that if he were involved in an attempt to somehow discredit me it was likely that he or his helpers had indeed left a clue at the barn. If so I thought I should examine the barn again in daylight, which meant early the next morning. Oddly enough, this would have been the time I would have returned from New York under the original plan, and knowing that I had not taken the chance to attack Coe left me with a good feeling, no matter what else was happening with the car and equipment.

Ready before dawn, I took the path through the woods yet again to the barn. While there I double-checked the spot where I had originally buried the equipment, carefully sifting the loose fine dirt. Finding nothing, I completed the cleaning, careful to leave no sign before returning to the camping area.

I was determined to act as normal as possible, so I called Rebecca when I returned, giving her the numbers I had promised from the now-staffed lodge. She sounded the same as always, as I hoped I did, and was glad to have a phone number from the office here instead of just the pay phone, which I had given her on Sunday. I said hello to a few folks while I walked to the lodge and back, though I dearly wished to know what was going on.

I was thoroughly confused. Even as I tried to tell myself that I couldn't possibly be in trouble now, my guilt was confusing my logic.

By the end of the day I had visited several people and their camps, trading business cards with some new friends, accepting the condolences and well-wishes of old friends and others that knew my situation. I had an interesting conversation about arrow weight and flight distance, and made sure two or three people I knew visited me at the RV, so they would know the way it was set up.

I dumped the paper map in a campfire as soon as the opportunity presented itself, stirring the remains until they were gone. I was sure a few more days' ashes would hide all traces of the paper. It was kind of sad, really, all that work gone.

I had wiped all locations out of the GPS receiver, but re-recorded new routes one, two, and three on the shooting ranges just to be sure, set new coordinates while visiting sites in a random fashion. Everything should have been as clean now, except for the car and its contents.

*It seemed like a lifetime since I'd seen my Melissa.*

I had gotten used to the sense of knowing over the years, sensing the intentions of others. Daily training in the art that was fostered over time by my yado sensei, I had gradually learned to use this power without allowing it to overwhelm me in a sea of the emotions of others. Indeed, I had been overloaded with the feelings of others at first, but had been reminded of an old kyudo saying—"While shooting you must be aware of the slightest breeze, yet not be disturbed by the thunder." Absorbing this knowledge helped me to realize that I had to always be aware of everything around me while discriminating between the things that required my attention and those that did not.

Melissa's side—that's where I belonged.

I called the hospital to find out her condition, then rounded up the kids. I needed to hug them all, hard.

*I was holding my baby's hand again, much sooner than I thought I would be. We were together again.*

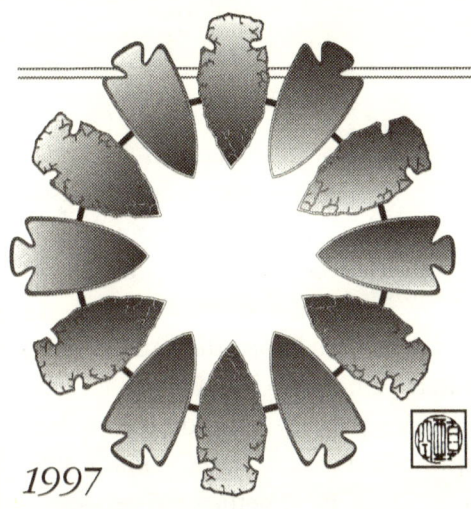

*1997*

# Kentucky

*I usually kept a long perspective on things, feeling life as an internal river that had no visible end, a flowing force that ran a true course, keeping me from sweating the small stuff.*

*As something discordant entered my stream and tried to distract me, it would many times be absorbed in the flow, diluted and joined.*

*I sat next to Melissa now, rubbing each muscle and joint in turn, trying to keep each part of her strong, lengthened, and flexible. I did this often, making sure I pressed a thumb to both ends of every muscle while trying to visualize a proper flow of energy. I paid special attention to her inner organs, manipulating the parts of her that were never really touched by others, massaging them deeply. By special permission I was the one who gave her the sponge baths that kept her clean, to wash the golden bright hair that lay in a long braid over the side of the bed.*

*Now that I had my time and concentration back I could do this more often, touching each part of her more intimately than I ever had when she was awake, when she could control her own body. I was careful to be aware of the flow, to let any little negative particles drop into my stream as it washed through her and back into me, keeping her pure. Her health and safe return to her family were the important things, the forever things— anything else was the small stuff now, and I had to remember that.*

It was time to tackle this thing, fully and with no reservations.

My attention was no longer split by Coe, Samantha, and Melissa. Samantha was gone, taken from me forever; Coe was gone from my life, hopefully, with the security I hired still in place; Melissa alone was not gone, but here, my center.

Granny Rebecca had been a rock, and was happy the situation was more in focus. We had decided not to have her take the children to Ohio this summer for their normal visit, but to keep them here and a part of their mother's possible recovery. Everything had settled into a comfortable, supportive routine, and I was now free to heal my sweetheart. The doctors were still skeptical, but they didn't know us, didn't know the stubborn people they were dealing with.

I had always been a problem-solver, applying myself to the concern at hand, using the same creative methods for making new paintings, fixing mechanical problems, altering life situations, whatever. I had faith—faith in my Missy, faith in God, faith in our love—and I was willing to give myself over completely to my faith, to solve this most important problem.

I believed that, in general, problems had to be handled in their own frameworks. A work of art to be painted as a sumi-e subject, for example, limited me to the ways that different concentrations of ink would flow onto very porous rice paper, and the only freedom from those restrictions would be my own level of skill. I accepted these restrictions when I painted because they gave me an environment in which to create something that had never been seen before, a focus within the accepted methods. This was different—we had already tried to heal my wife using the framework of skilled health professionals using modern medical science, and it hadn't worked very well.

Larger problems required larger answers.

*After working on Melissa, I paced back and forth in the room, trying to list possibilities, no matter how remote. If there were a potential answer I wanted to find it.*

*I listed the possibilities once again. Her coma was not caused by anything physical, and was not maintained by anything we could scientifically detect. She even appeared relatively healthy because of the care she was receiving.*

*She showed signs of wanting to come out of it, little twitches and squeezes that showed me she was waiting, wanting to come back. The responses were not automatic, I thought, but conscious. The reactions I got from her occurred when I talked to her, when I tried to connect with her on subjects she cared about.*

*How could I help create those connections more consistently? If I could reach her more often, maybe those little reactions would come more frequently, perhaps even bring her closer to the surface.*

*Perhaps if she felt my hand leading her to the light she would have the strength to follow.*

I had to make some assumptions here.

I had to think she was still aware, still the bright and sensitive woman I married so long ago. If she was aware and mentally functioning at some level, it must be the fear of facing the horror of Samantha's mutilation and death (if she indeed knew that Sam died) that was keeping her away from the world, despite her small reactions.

So how would I reach her? How could I cross that thin barrier that separated us each from the other?

I knew there must be some way to merge with her, to contact her and bring her back—what I didn't know was how. Talking alone wasn't working well enough even when it was her husband, mother, father, and children that were the ones talking to her, so there must be some additional way.

How does one person invade another? How does one being connect to another? I didn't want to limit the possibilities, and didn't care how fantastic the list became—I would consider anything.

Over the next several days I worked on my problem, making a mental list of all the possibilities I could, even keeping a pad next to the bed to capture ideas that came in the night.

I started a very special set of arrows as a focal point, working on them for hours each evening, letting my mind rest in concentration.

*Sex, of course, was an important way to connect with another person, and had been a strong unifying point for us in the past. It was one way to reflect love, probably the strongest bond we shared, and a bond reinforced with any caring form of touch.*

*Electricity or some sort of magnetic field went on the list as well, some power, some bridge—maybe even some computer connection.*

*An act of violence was the most direct way to invade someone else, of course—I had to include that. There was also the personal interaction of a psychologist or psychiatrist, even though that required conscious communication—or did it?*

*There were intellectual discussions, responses to art or music or books or dancing, even asking questions to invoke a response—the list grew as I tried to find the clue or clues.*

I sat on her bed at about the level of her knees, looking at her gentle face. If I could just communicate directly with her I knew I could comfort her, really relate to her, wake her, bring her back, no matter if I had to try a thousand times.

Settling myself, I picked up her left hand and placed it across mine in a loose grasp with my fingers up on her wrist, feeling her warmth.

I slowly closed my eyes as I straightened my back, wanting to merge myself with her world. I felt her heart beating in her wrist and slowed my own to match hers, something that would have alarmed the doctors if they had measured it then. We had done this many times before the accident, matching each other's heartbeat, matching each other's breath—it was something natural to us both. Even if her own heartbeat was unnaturally slow now, I wanted a middle ground and was willing to meet her wherever I had to go.

I sat in the inner darkness for a long time, waiting for my sweetheart, beating with her, breathing with her.

I visualized us together, just holding each other—I tried to really feel her holding me, her arms comforting me, her self real and fully alive again, her spark regained. I felt her ki next to mine, something even more familiar to me than the sight of her face, the face I loved so much. The connection of our inner lives appealed to a much more real and basic sense than the sense of sight and was something I trusted much more than my own eyes.

Suddenly something changed. Not only did I sense a slight squeeze from her hand and a slight change in her breathing, but looking through half-closed eyes I saw her eyes move side-to-side beneath their lids as if in REM sleep. I cried then, resting my head on her hand, rubbing it tenderly.

The sense of her was so real to me now that I welcomed the tears, but didn't want to do anything that might break this spell. I concentrated on our connection, then on visualizing each feature in turn, not only the features I had seen and felt over the years but the internal features I had studied while she was in bed—the muscles, nerves, and synapses, the only parts of her I had really known during the last long months. I didn't know whether these things I was experiencing were real or imagined, but for the moment I didn't care.

*My Christian roots were grown strong and deep. I had always felt the teachings of Christ himself to be the important concern, and had concentrated on the four Gospels rather than the interpretations that followed in other books.*

*It was perhaps my deepest-held belief that Christ meant for us to achieve his perfection and to be able to live as he lived, to perform his miracles, to bring heaven on earth—a hurtful admission, when I remembered what I had been willing to do to my enemy just a short time ago.*

*Everything Christ had done seemed to have been to bring us closer together. Casting out demons that kept us from our true selves, demanding that we lead full lives that bore fruit for others, speaking in tongues to communicate between one another, and of course, most important to me now, healing, making whole.*

*When I was young I had been taught that when Christ spoke to us about "having the faith of a mustard seed" he was choosing the smallest living thing available to emphasize the reality of the tiny amount of faith needed to heal. When I pondered the nature of this tiny seed, though, it struck me that the mustard seed, or any other living thing, could only follow its own unique nature—a mustard seed had no choice but to grow into a mustard tree. If Christ was telling us that this power to heal was part of our own nature then—if we weren't distracted—we fully contained the power to heal naturally and easily.*

*I believed in the law, odd though that may have sounded now. I didn't mean man-made laws, though, for I considered those to be rules, and rules can be broken. A law to me was a law of the universe, something that could not be broken. Gravity was a true law, a fact that we had to acknowledge whether we wished to or not. Healing, if I was correct, was also a true law and something available to us all, a law in fact whose existence was only less recognized than gravity. The access to healing, then, was only determined by our point of view, the recognition of its availability as a law of nature.*

*Since laws were universal, that meant the understanding of the law showed us the truth, the way things really were, universally.*

*I had, in a sense, begun to merge with some universal truths through kyudo, so decided to add this belief to my study on a daily basis, for that had always been my method of attempting perfection, no matter how far short of the goal I fell. I had always heard it said that "practice makes perfect," and whatever laws I was realizing through kyudo were my normal and habitual attempt at perfection.*

*What many people don't realize, though, is that it is only perfect practice that makes perfect.*

We worked with Melissa for hours every day, cajoling her with stimuli, caring for her in every way possible.

I found a psychiatrist who was willing to counsel Melissa, even though it would mean a one-way conversation. I wasn't allowed in the room during the sessions, but hoped for any little improvement from quasi-interaction with an objective and caring counselor. This was a new technique and one more means of support.

*In the hospital room I sat with Melissa, holding her hand. I saw us through my eyes, walking together in the sculpture garden she loved so deeply, saw her freed from the bed, moving her own beautiful legs. I felt the sun, heard the birds, smelled the breeze, tasted our happiness, walked with her. It seemed as though it was real.*

*I wanted her to act on her own, to want to walk beside me, so I imagined myself letting go of her hand to walk next to me without touching. She looked at me and laughed her little laugh, then picked up my right hand and kissed my palm. She studied my hand as she held it and walked, then thoughtfully put it back in her own hand.*

*We walked along and I talked to her about small things, holding hands like the lovers we were. I tried to see each part of her, to feel her, to smell her, to remember her, to make her as real as possible. I wanted desperately to communicate with her, to show her how I felt. I reminded her we were close to home and told her I missed her deeply—wouldn't she come home?*

*Of her own volition she stopped, turned to face me. Now I was able to fully bring her beautiful face into focus, and I watched as it changed, showing not only her features but her intentions and emotions as well. I saw her ambivalent desire to be back in the world with me and with us, her fear about coming to grips with Sam's death. A range of emotions and thoughts crossed her face, each as clear as a large billboard to me, each changing her emotional landscape. Finally I saw her reluctantly give up any attempt to explain, saw her dismiss the subject from her mind.*

*She looked deeply into my eyes, then to her index fingertip as she brought it up between our faces. I looked at her finger where she held it, then watched as she touched it to her forehead. The spot glowed as I watched, fascinated. When she removed her finger the tip of it held the glow, and I stood transfixed as she moved it towards me.*

*As she touched my forehead I felt a web of energy move through me, starting with a golden-warm pressure on my skin that spread over my skull, then a deeper wave of love and pressure flowed through every part of my brain in turn. I felt it involve my outer brain and then the inner cortexes, merging deeply with my instinctive self. I felt a surge of warmth and light as this power merged at a point at the base of my skull, then flashed through my whole body, lighting me like an incandescent bulb, healing me. The light settled in my ki, warming me, letting me know everything would be all right.*

*I opened my eyes as the nurse turned on the bedside lamp, relieving the new twilight. I saw the look of pity in her eyes, but could also read her face the way I had read Missy's just moments before. I saw she believed I had a morbid fascination with my wife. It was not an accusation, but a concern, and I could see it in her as easily as I could tell the color of her brown eyes. Her face was like a symphony of thoughts, thoughts obvious to me.*

*I had continued to hold my baby's hand and I looked at her face, unmoving now as it had been for so long. I could still read her face as I had in the vision, but it was faint, wispy. Her eyes were slightly opened, glistening in the lamplight.*

*After a few minutes I squeezed her hand, feeling and looking to see if there would be a response, disappointed when it didn't come. Something had changed, though, I could feel it and see it. There was a changed awareness in me.*

After some time I said good-bye to Melissa, kissing her on the forehead and looking at her face one more time, then went to the cafeteria, watching the people I passed, seeing each person with a heightened awareness, reading their thoughts, feeling their concerns. Each face told a story, some that involved me, some that didn't, but most had a need for healing that I could now feel.

*This was new ability, an addition to the power to read intentions, and the two flowed together as if they belonged. Each step I took felt unique, each breath full and vibrant.*

*An important part of Christ's teaching had been that healing could only flow from one to another when both believed and accepted, and a part of me now saw not only the need for healing, but knew when someone was ready to receive. When I knew it would help, I allowed the healing energy to flow, boundless in its depths—I seemed connected to it all.*

*I felt like I was trying to drive down a road that had stop signs at every intersection. Each person I encountered was no longer just another random being that could be disregarded as they happened to cross my path, but rather an involvement, an open book that could not be ignored.*

*I was amazed at the range of emotions I witnessed. Now in the main part of the medical center, I saw many different stories—a new grandparent here, a new orphan there, stories of worry and concern everywhere. I started to walk slowly, trying to absorb what was happening to me, every new person's story involving me in their lives, their deepest hearts.*

A hospital might not have been the best place to discover this new awareness, a building filled mainly with personal tragedies, but I hadn't had a choice. Deciding not to eat here, I left—I could at least choose to do that.

I had an hour to think and absorb on the way home, an hour alone in the dark on country roads.

*The house was quiet and darkened when I arrived, but my day was far from over.*

*I took the unstrung Japanese bow down from its pegs above the swords and wiped it lovingly with a clean soft cloth, slowly, noting its carefully constructed details.*

*This wasn't my original yumi but one I had gotten last year from a master maker in the southern island of Kyushu. It sometimes calmed me to care for my yumi—it would calm me more to shoot it, but there wasn't time for that now.*

*I noted the yellowish and figured beauty of the waxwood used for the tips and for the laminations on the outer edge and how it so easily complemented the yellow of the bamboo used on the front and back. The white suede leather grip was wearing in nicely and I noted how it was darkening, the smooth pattern my repeated grip was leaving on it.*

*My den-office was a good place to have this bow, a constant reminder of my heritage—real and assumed—as I played with the computers and cared for my family and business. It had a place of honor above the daikatana, the long sword, and above the saber that had belonged to my great-grandfather. It always seemed strange to me that just three generations separated me from the Civil War, something I thought about occasionally.*

*My thoughts now were on a time not quite as far back as that, though. I was remembering the summer after high school.*

*I worked as an artist for the Florida Division of what was then called H.E.W.—Health, Education, and Welfare. I liked my boss, an African-American lady who was an intelligent and caring person.*

*I had been having precognitive dreams for a while then, dreams that showed me small things that would happen a day or two later. I didn't have them often or usually remember them, but when the reality happened it would overlay the dream so thoroughly that I immediately knew what was going to happen next. This had been going on for quite some time, and I had been counting on those dreams, reassured somehow they were good things leading to a certain future.*

*The part of the H.E.W. building where I worked was new but crowded, with a wide desk-lined hallway leading back to my boss's office. The entrance to my work area led off the right side of the hallway about halfway down, a rather crowded space with a desk, drawing board, and various supply shelves. I enjoyed working there, and I think many of the full-fledged adults enjoyed my playful work habits. I remembered a lot about that summer because I gained a number of production skills, even still used some of them.*

*I had been outside next to the back stairs taking 35mm photographs of calligraphically drawn title cards to be turned into a slide presentation for the field workers. I had run out of film so had come back in to get more, and as I entered the hallway I saw my boss standing next to her desk. I decided to walk back to talk for a few minutes—we liked each other, and I always kept up with my work load, so she never had to push me to meet my deadlines.*

*As I walked forward the overlay of a dream hit me full in the face—I had lived this before.*

*I remembered each micro-event of the dream, the way every person moved, who was on the phone saying what, how the chairs were arranged—everything. I knew when I walked closer to her office I would see her slip and hurt herself badly. I realized it for a certainty, had seen it happen—I even knew which bone in her wrist she would break.*

*Without thinking I turned right into my office instead of walking straight ahead, then listened fearfully while standing close to the doorway. After several minutes it became obvious that nothing unusual had happened and everything was all right, so I got the film and went back outside to finish my shooting.*

*I can't say for sure whether anything would have happened to her that day, but I had known it would at the time and that's what mattered—the dream had warned me, and I knew I had saved someone I cared about from a painful injury.*

*The only thing that had happened with certainty that day was the loss of my special dreams—I never had another.*

*That event of long ago reminded me of my loss then, and it worried me that the healing power I felt now might leave as suddenly, but I forced myself to rest in the knowledge I now carried.*

I didn't want to know what every person I came in contact with was thinking—far from it—but if I did anything to reject this gift I might be losing a tool I could use to help Melissa. I hoped it might be something I could learn to control, but I felt I would just have to ride with it until I got used to the extent of this new sight. All I wanted was to heal my baby, to have her back home.

For all I knew I wouldn't have this special sight in the morning, that it would fade away like a dream, but if that happened it would be beyond my control, and I couldn't do without sleep. The only thing I knew for sure now was that I couldn't risk doing anything purposely that might cut it off.

When I was in Japan I was told about the difference between Oriental and Occidental babies, illustrated for me by a young mother. The lady showing me this was speaking quietly while watching over her young daughter. The baby was asleep, breathing quietly through her nose. I watched as her mother reached down and gently pinched her nose closed, cutting off her air. After a moment the child opened her mouth to breathe, barely breaking her sleep-rhythm. "You see," she said, "many gaijin babies would wake up crying, probably scared."

Perhaps it was time for me to breathe through my mouth until I got used to things.

I re-placed the unstrung yumi on its pegs, ends facing downward as etiquette required.

I visited each child in turn, reading their sleeping faces. Fifteen, twelve, and ten years old now, Jessica, Hanna, and Markie all carried concern on their faces, concern that made them appear older, even in sleep. I tried to touch inside each one, to allow them to rest completely. I visited Rebecca's open doorway next, silently calming her fears about her daughter and her grandchildren from a distance—she had been such a rock through all this.

I set myself to awaken early enough to fix breakfast for them all—I wanted to see their faces with my new awareness.

I awoke alone, of course, but with some thought or dream remembrance I tried to capture, a ghost image that had just been clear to me a moment before. An urge to pee forced the thought out of my mind, as so often happens, and the ghost faded away.

As I returned to the bedroom I sat myself in a meditation pose, immediately noticing that I felt generally much more at peace with myself than I had in recent memory. I somehow felt I was internally integrating this new ability of mine, but I wanted to rest with it now, to assure myself I could handle the press of the many faces I would be seeing, today and hopefully every day.

My fear that this sight would leave me during the night had been unfounded—I didn't have to read a face to know it hadn't left me, because it changed the way I saw and felt everything.

I still had an hour before everyone was due to get up, so I made Belgian waffles for everyone, keeping them warm in the oven on their own plates as each was done. It seemed like it had been forever since I used this recipe.

*Hanna popped her head in early, probably awakened by the smell.*

*"Hey, Daddy, what are you doing?"*

*"Good morning, Bunkin, just making breakfast before I go to the hospital."*

*I turned to face her, a little worried at what might be there. What I saw was a beautiful girl on the cusp of womanhood, a kind person who loved her family and friends, an intelligent and creative person who worried a great deal about me and about her mother.*

*"Daddy, don't you think I'm a little old to be called 'bunkin?'"*

*I held my arms out for a deep hug, feeling her beautiful self merge with mine.*

After a few moments I replied "Never, my Little One—you'll always be a bunkin to me. If it bothers you, though, I'll try to remember not to call you that." I was feeling our connection so strongly. I held her tightly, feeling her wonderful nature, feeling our relationship. Her head topped my shoulder now—she really was growing up.

After a moment she began to cry and held me more tightly while she released. What's the matter?" I asked automatically.

"Oh, Daddy, I'm so worried."

She sobbed against my shoulder for several minutes, then let it pour out, telling me how miserable she had been because of her mother and Samantha, how she worried about me, how she was afraid we would never be happy again, never be a real family. She purged herself of many things, then, emotions she had held inside far too long. Her sister and mother had been ripped from her, and she had sensed how deeply I had changed, perhaps lost to her as well.

As she cried I maintained my connection with her, feeling her pain, healing her. When she was done I washed her face with warm water and a soft towel, knowing even these small fatherly things might not be welcomed too much longer by this, the family's newest young lady.

I let her eat, spending more time with her, telling her of some of the things I was going to try. "There really is a chance she's going to be okay, Hanna—would you like your Grandmother to bring you to the hospital later?"

"Sure, Dad, I'd like that."

"Okay, I'll check to make sure everybody else wants to go, too, so nobody'll be left alone, but it should be okay—we should all be able to go."

She ate while she babbled on about things happening in school, what her friends were up to, how the new colt was doing. It was like a cork had been popped out of a bottle, letting a spray of her little life cover everything in sight, a life I had forcibly removed myself from several months ago.

I finally chased her upstairs to get ready. When the waffles were all done and warming, I went upstairs to awaken the other kids. They both were able to sense my change and clung to me as if they hadn't seen me in so very long, especially Jessica. I hadn't realized how alone they all felt, how abandoned, and I knew I had to be there for them from now on.

I hadn't handled this situation very well.

Memories were funny, I knew, made of many things. A feeling that connoted the weather, an impression of background noises, wisps of a small smell, the hiccup of a laugh, the warmth of a touch, the visual *remembrance of an event—all these pieces fit together to form a ball that is our memory of an event. I knew I wouldn't forget my children as I saw them now, that each small piece of the individuals that they were would stay with me forever.*

*The hospital trip was fine with everyone's schedule, so that was done. I wanted more time with them now, more time to enjoy their company.*

*I would do this more often now, I thought, while I could. I knew as they grew older there wouldn't be as much room for me—they would soon start on their own paths to their separate lives. Then and only then would we see how well we had done as parents, my Melissa and me.*

*It had always been important for me to enjoy life's basic joys, and I had been ignoring this one, the simple love and concern for my babies. It always amazed me that what the eye could see would change what the ear could hear—their pain had been awaiting my acknowledgment for so long, and I could see it now, no longer able to ignore the suffering and longing I had been blind to.*

*I was even able to get Rebecca to release to me, this stoic woman who had kept my family together. I owed her so much—how could I have withdrawn so far from these special people who supported me so well in my time of grief?*

*Never again.*

In the next several weeks we all became a team, working together to heal Missy. I didn't bring the children to the medical center often—just enough to let them feel involved in the process. I didn't think it was a good idea for them to see her day after day, to see all the baby steps. I knew children had a shorter view of time and expected my enthusiasm to yield instantaneous results, so I didn't want to overtax their expectations. We talked about it every day now, though—we were all involved. I spent much more time at home with the children and Rebecca, being very careful not to slip back into my obsessive ways.

I had special times of the day I would spend in communion with my sweetheart, and I felt our connection grow over time, felt her come to depend on our contact, rejoiced in each small inner step she took.

She was responding more frequently now, small squeezes with her hand and more eye movement, but she still refused to come all the way back.

I gradually felt more comfortable with my new sight, solidifying the ability to read and heal while integrating it into my way of looking at the world. I learned a great deal about people now, learned something new from each person I met, and each thing I learned I carried back to my darling.

While I worked with her to heal, I tried new methods of drawing her out.

I read to her, of course, as did we all, but we did more than that. There was now a DVD-connected Macintosh on her tray table—Apple's limited-edition twentieth anniversary *Spartacus* model with a bright color LCD screen and a TV tuner—placed where she could see it easily.

We made sure there was material in front of her every day on a strictly-timed schedule so she could come to anticipate it, always assuming she knew it was there. We filled the screen with her favorite shows, music videos, travelogues, and home videos, both those familiar to her as well as new ones. Her reactions were monitored and we were gradually able to recognize patterns that indicated her interest level.

One of the monitoring techniques measured eye movement. Since her eyes were slightly open most of the time, we were able to measure when she might actually be watching something on the screen, using that as an indication of interest, and we were getting measurable results. We could see interest on her face when we had a "hit," further confirming our results. She was showing much more activity now.

I never let any of these new techniques deter me from her inner healing, of course, but spent many hours matched with her, hand in hand.

Over time we introduced items I thought would draw her out, debates on subjects I knew she had passion for, and we varied those with more soothing subjects.

I had one major project at the house, now. I was going to put up a new building on top of the hill overlooking the sculpture garden. I was having recurring dreams about the twelve-sided white chamber and made a special point to note design elements whenever I saw it. I didn't know its significance, but knew it was somehow important to me.

I had always laughed when someone said they gave more than a hundred percent, but it was true for me now. It wasn't that I was physically capable of more than 100% effort—more like a total accumulation of factors that reflected more than just physical effort. It was the push I was giving, true, but it was also the planning, the tools, the accumulated knowledge, the creativity—everything together.

*There were so many people working to help my sweetheart—extremely capable people working together. It was like bits of wind joining with each other to become a whirlwind, a force powerful enough to accomplish anything.*

I suspected Melissa now of playing games with me, of being more ready to come back than she would admit, perhaps of getting a little complacent. I had tried to create an island for her, a place of stimulation and security, and might have done too well. She might very well be happy there, not having to face her fears, and since I purposely stayed away from any mention of little Samantha she might be willing to live in her solitary world for whatever future she could foresee.

I thought perhaps I could trick her, use her ever-repeating schedule to bring her the last little step back to us.

I carefully considering exactly how to fool her, to help her through the last part of her journey. After setting the stage for days, I was ready to try.

During the replay of a favorite video well after dark, I deliberately had the sight, sound, and room lights turned off at the same instant, cutting off all stimuli at once.

I thought I heard a little whimper as I squeezed her hand and said, "Missy? Are you okay, sweetheart?" I tried to sound just as I would have if she had been upset while lying in our own bed.

"What happened?" She asked, weakly.

"Oh, baby, is it really you?" I grabbed her hand firmly but gently.

"Why are the lights out?" She sounded so confused.

"Sweetheart, oh, Melissa!" I had difficulty breathing. I leaned up and rested my cheek against hers to feel her now-awake warmth, still holding her hand. She might be teetering on the brink, ready to either fall back in or land safely on the outside, and I felt the need to be careful.

"Marcus, I feel so weak... why are the lights out?"

"Baby, you've had a little problem, and you're in the hospital."

"What happened?"

"Don't worry about it now, Sweetheart? Just talk to me for a few minutes, okay, and tell me things, just to let me hear your voice—I've missed you so very much."

*She was back—weak and disoriented, but back.*

We brought her fully back over the next few days, gently returning her to the world that had taken her baby. It was a gentle and careful process—emotionally as well as physically. We spent long hours talking and touching, and the rest of the family helped get her back on the road to becoming the loving and full person she had been before. We were all so happy now, and couldn't wait to bring her home, something we had been wanting for a long time.

She still spent long hours viewing various media on the *Spartacus*, but loved the books most of all. I gradually weaned her from wanting us to read to her, making her use her own inner and outer muscles as much as possible, helping her regain her strength.

I used books, magazines, and stories as rewards for successful physical therapy sessions, at least until she accused me of acting more like a doctor than a husband. I mentally had to switch gears again, for I had become like a doctor to her over a period of months, but now had to learn to be her mate once again, to treat her as a woman.

The doctors were amazed, of course, studying her as much as I would let them. I apologized for any inappropriate behavior, for I knew some of the nurses resented my continual presence.

*I was examining one of my favorite bows, an English longbow made by a famous maker from Alaska. Fifty-five pounds at a twenty-nine and a half inch draw, it was smooth and sweet.*

*The bow was seventy-five inches long, made from Cascade Yew cut from trees that grew at an elevation of four thousand feet. Trees that high matured slowly, making very thin growth rings, yielding a bow that had a lot of strength and stability. The tips were made from light-colored horn, exquisitely carved, and the burgundy leather for the grip had been beveled on the back edge before being wrapped, giving it a rounded and sculptured feel. In a slight departure from tradition, the light sapwood back was covered with a layer of rawhide, the white layer making the bow even stronger.*

*Every time I saw this bow I admired the velvet-like appearance of its finish, each thin ring adding to its grace and beauty.*

*I warmed up for a while then set up a couple of English games to match my mood. I shot wands at a hundred yards for a while, six-foot dry sticks simply poked in the ground in front of earthen backstops, the only goal to "split the wand." Then I shot targets at that distance, the standard international forty-eight inch faces reducing from a large outer white ring down to black, to blue, to red, then to a center ring of gold. Traditionally, the size of the prize depended on how close to the center the ring hit was, the golden center ring paying the most.*

*Scoring this way revealed a difference in philosophy between traditional and target archery. A target that only registered a first hit showed the paper target represented a live being which would be killed by an arrow, instead of being a simple repetitive scoring device.*

*I had know outdoor shooters over the years that were extremely accurate at unknown distances on uncertain terrain, and I had known extremely accurate indoor target shooters who placed a shaft almost in the same hole time after time, but seldom did the two cross over. There was some internal difference, some way of thinking that varied in the two types of archer. I suppose the reason I enjoyed both types of shooting related to my Japanese training—shooting at a target while becoming a part of it, making it a part of me. The target wasn't there to be scored like paper, but to be connected with like a live target.*

*I considered a plan to place English stone "roving marks" at various places on my property to make a shooting course. Usually made of carved stone, the marks had large deep holes drilled in their tops to hold a wand or other wooden device—a target. Each mark was named, which I liked, and the distances between them could vary from twenty yards to well over two hundred. When shooting with more than one person the one who hit closest to the mark picked the next target, so the course would vary each time it was shot.*

*Roving marks were used for at least a century after guns replaced bows on the battlefield as practice for hunting, still the domain of the bow. Game was considered "noble quarry," a fit target for a broadhead tipped arrow, long after a not-so-noble human adversary could be shot with a gun on a battlefield.*

*There was also a recreated Magyar bow made by an Hungarian bowmaker, another person deeply concerned with reviving mounted archery. A short bow with long static ears, it was an amazing bow, even though it was made out of primarily modern materials. I enjoyed shooting this bow—when I shot the longbows I always felt as though there was a little "bounce" missing, some vibration my hand expected that never came. This bow was different, though—I could see myself shooting this bow from horseback, riding down a row of targets to strike them one after another. The grip had a slab of horn on either side that the arrow slid across, a departure from the padded surfaces I was used to. This was fun! Much less delicate than its sinew-wrapped authentic counterpart, I would love this bow in the woods.*

*Each shot from each bow had such a wonderful lesson to give, and I was blessed to live in the time that bridged the old and the new. Traditional materials like ivory were common when I was young, even though expensive, but were disappearing now because of too-great demands placed on elephants—a ban well-justified. At the same time, modern developments like carbon-fiber limbs and fast flight synthetic bowstrings were boosting the performance levels of even the most traditional bows. While we were just beginning to rediscover the secrets of bow designs a thousand years old, computer-aided design was wringing the most out of their modern counterparts.*

*I lived in an era that spanned the ages from flint arrowheads to permanently sharp ceramic knife blades, and I loved it, especially since my own life bridged the gap between the old and new arts, now and forever.*

*Much like deciding which bow to use, I was beginning to try to decide how much of my healing art I had the responsibility to share now that I didn't have to concentrate solely on my wife. Could it be shared? Was it possible just because of my relationship with my wife?*

A few nights later as I was leaving the center and a sleeping Missy, walking down the now familiar hall to the entrance, I stopped in my tracks. A middle-aged Japanese gentleman was coming towards me, looking directly into my eyes.

I couldn't read him! His face was the first I had seen since I gained my new sight that was just a face, no messages, no desires, no healing needs. He walked up to me, bowed, gave me his card, and shook my hand, introducing himself and giving the code phrase that identified him as a yado practitioner, a phrase I hadn't heard in a long time.

Yoshimoro sensei spoke to me there in the hall, then we went out to the parking lot. I didn't think there were many about who spoke Japanese, but still didn't want to take the chance of being overheard.

"Hiroshu sensei sends his regards, Maaku-san, and says to tell you he has missed you."

"And I him, sensei. I have missed his counsel—it's been impossible to visit this year."

"Sensei is aware of your situation, and is worried about you. He hopes perhaps your entire family can visit for a few weeks once your wife feels up to it."

"Sensei has often reconsidered his distaste for the telephone, but still feels he is better off only speaking to people face-to-face. Please rest assured that he has kept an eye on you and your family, especially your wife's miraculous healing. He and I, as well as all your friends in Japan grieve with you for the loss of your daughter."

"Thank you, sensei."

"Maaku-san, I'm sure you were made aware of some of the things a higher-level student can accomplish—didn't some of the stories indicate a heightened awareness, a different way of seeing?"

"Of course, but I thought this sight came from my connection to my wife—I never connected it to kyudo or yado."

"It may have come from your desire to help your wife, but you may rest assured it might not have come at all if you had not studied our arts. One of the basics of Zen training is the direct transmission of knowledge, but there is nothing to say it always has to come from a sensei. As you know, we are taught to put our learning into practice, and to study the world around us—evidently you learned that lesson.

"However, it is only one lesson out of many.

"If you could gain that sight, wouldn't you guess someone who trained daily with a sensei might gain many things? There are many senses, after all."

"Does this mean that sensei always knew what I was thinking while I was studying with him?"

"Of course."

"Oh."

"Any sensei sees things the student doesn't realize he sees, so please don't worry.

"Sensei is worried now that your training has become what you call lop-sided, that you have trained alone for too long, that you have learned a great deal about some things, too little about others.

"He wishes you would consider studying yado back in Japan with him, when things settle down for you."

"But..."

"Please—don't answer now. You have a busy time ahead of you."

"Yes, Yoshimoro sensei. Would you care to visit my home? I would like very much to speak more with you, perhaps even to practice yado together—it has been a long time since I have had a teacher."

"I would enjoy that a great deal, but it might be better if I waited until you are less busy. I will contact you in a few weeks—is that all right?"

"Certainly, sensei. Do you live in this country?"

"Oh, no. I am a businessman who has to visit many places in the world frequently, so sometimes has the duty to keep an eye on various children that are scattered about, such as you. I have been here before."

"Thank you—I appreciate your concern. Are there many of us throughout the world?"

"Enough, though your situation is unique."

"Sensei, can you tell me why you picked this time to contact me, not earlier or later?"

"Yes, of course Maaku-san. Hiroshu sensei wanted me to warn you."

"Warn me? Of what?"

"Let me ask you a question, if I may: Do you know why there is so little crime in Japan, Maaku-san?"

"Well, it's common knowledge the Japanese are very law-abiding."

"Ah—but why?"

"A respect for authority? I must admit I'm guessing, sensei—I don't really know."

"Let me tell you, then—it is because of this: If a man broke in to the house of another, or stole from someone, then that criminal would create a karmic relationship with his victim—an obligation if you will, one to tie both the thief and his family with the victim and his. Many times this sets numerous events into motion, and complicates lives that already have many legitimate obligations. Life would quickly become much too complex for any *Nippongin* that disregarded this universal law.

"In other words, Maaku-san, even if we feel we are justified in taking an action, we may be setting up events we can't control, and even the lowest would-be criminal realizes that."

"I don't understand, Yoshimoro sensei."

"In simplest terms it means that you must concentrate the skills you have, focusing them very carefully. You will need training—again."

1998

*Honshu*

Standing on the line, I drew the fast flight bowstring on the forty-six pound Hoyt Avalon target recurve bow, anchoring just beside my chin. The complex AVRS stabilizer system waved slightly, then stilled.

I consciously checked the thousand details of my shot while concentrating on the alignment of the small circle and pin sight extending from the front of the bow. If my form was absolutely consistent and if the pieces and parts of the bow and attached gear were in perfect mechanical sync with each other, the pin should accurately reflect where the arrow would hit at ninety meters. If my release was perfect. If I correctly judged the wind.

I held the string with a Cavalier tab, a synthetic leather, metal, and composite release device that had a shelf designed to rest up against the lower edge of my jaw, a tab custom fitted to my hand. The tip of the Easton X10 aluminum/carbon shaft rested just under the light metal lip of the clicker—when the point of the shaft pulled back past it, the lip would slip past the arrow's tip, hitting against the riser. If I released just at the moment I heard that "click" then my draw length should be exactly the same for each shot.

As I paused at full draw I reflected for a moment, then gradually pulled my shoulder blades together ever-so-slightly to draw the arrow the last fraction of an inch until I heard the clicker. My fingers flicked just the smallest amount when the string released, sending the arrow in a shallow arc to the distant target.

*I held my position for a few seconds after the arrow hit the target and assessed the shot on both physical and spiritual levels. I centered, appreciating the connection I had with the bow, the arrow, the target. My heart and respiration rates dropped as I performed my meditation, shot after shot.*

*It was important for me to shoot all of my bows. I often found that a small bit of knowledge gained from one shooting style would help with another—it also bothered me to own a bow and not take care of it or shoot it, probably the only restraint on the number of bows I acquired.*

*This was essentially the same equipment used in the Atlanta Olympic Games and was a combination of high-tech marvels. I had picked a medium wrist twenty-five inch riser anodized in Black Splash, a color that matched the Carbon Plus Limbs, the X10 arrows, and the AVRS stabilizer system. Target recurve archery advances tend to be announced just before each Olympic four year cycle, and the technical advances that drive the modern target recurve bow fed back and forth with the advances in compound bows. This was currently the apex of modern recurve design, in my opinion, and there was no doubt it was a well-made piece of equipment.*

*Archery had to be dropped from the Olympics after the 1920 Games because each country insisted on its own rules and format. It was readmitted in 1972, forty-one years after the founding of the Federation Internationale De Tir a l'Arc, FITA, now the governing body of international archery competition with one hundred eight member countries. They introduced competition standards in their first year for all types of contests, persisting until enough countries had adopted their standards for international competition. While compounds seem to intrigue most shooters in the United States, there is no doubt target recurves have more practitioners worldwide.*

*After practice I unstrung the bow and placed it on its stand next to one of my yumi, by contrast simple, elegant, and muted—a harmonious expression of the traditional bowyer's art.*

*The bows themselves expressed the differences in their shooting styles, and I liked seeing them next to each other. While a shooter's form was critical to either style, the Olympic archers relied more on mechanically tuned equipment than the kyudo practitioners who were more concerned with combining the more spirit-involved aspects of Truth, Goodness, and Beauty.*

*Western archery judges competence by objective scores, although it's amazingly difficult sometimes to tell whether or not an arrow has cut into the next highest scoring ring. Kyudo has no such restrictions, judging the honor of shooting at each release. To combine the two forms of shooting was an amazing process.*

*M*elissa and the children had accompanied me to Japan before, many times, but this was our first trip since the accident—my wife was well again, looking forward to the visit.

The kids loved these trips. They loved the language, the people, the landscape, the animals, the stores: A trip like this was an adventure, an excuse for everyone to excitedly brush up on their Japanese language and etiquette, an experience they treasured.

While we were all shopping, Jessica, now sixteen, saw a gaijin loudly insisting that a store clerk speak to her in English. When she pointed out the tourist to me, I put my right arm around her and bent down to whisper in her ear, careful not to slow us down as we passed the inexcusable exchange at the sales counter.

"What do they call someone who speaks many languages?" I straightened up.

She looked up at me and spoke softly. "Multilingual?" A frown creased her tan forehead.

"Right." I smiled at her and quickly squeezed her shoulder, then bent down again.

"And what do they call someone who speaks two languages?"

She didn't skip a beat. "Bilingual?"

"Right again." Another squeeze, then I dropped my arm.

"So—what do they call someone who only speaks one language?"

She stopped, frowning again. I continued walking for a few paces, then turned to face her.

"I give," she said.

I walked closer to her, then bent over to whisper. "An American."

*The brothers J. Maurice and William H. Thompson became two of the founding members of the National Archery Association, the NAA, when it began in 1879. Their practice of archery began after the Civil War, a time when Confederates were not allowed to use firearms, and their practice grew to a passion over the years. Maurice wrote* The Witchery of Archery, *first published in 1878, a slim volume given credit by many for the rise of interest in archery in the United States at the beginning of the twentieth century, a time that saw the birth of many of the archers that have become our modern legends.*

*Each country has its own governing body affiliated with FITA, a function filled in the U.S. by the NAA.*

*Just as there are differences between kyudo and Olympic target archery that are expressed by their equipment and shooting styles, so are there apparent differences in their training and ranking systems.*

*There are five levels of instructor status in the NAA, the fifth being primarily honorary. If a student of archery wishes to participate in the Olympics it is imperative to first study with a Level Four national instructor, then to gain points through winning local, state, regional, national, and world competitions. A student's status is unofficial and fluctuates with a "what have you done for me lately" system of victories.*

*In modern kyudo there are numbered ranks corresponding to the "black belts" of other martial arts, up to the Tenth-Dan, with the ninth and tenth honorarily awarded. The sensei determines when a student is ready to be tested for a higher rank, and there are two tests—a written test and a shooting test—administered by the association. Sensei carry these rankings as well—instructor, teacher, master (also honorary)—although I would not presume to ever ask a sensei which rank he had earned.*

*If a student of archery wants to gain status in the world of kyudo it is imperative to understand that the benefits gained are internal, for there are few competitions and no way to become well-known outside your own circle. The process is not designed to promote personal glory, and even a public display of the art may only be appreciated by those who understand the beauty of a single perfectly-released shot.*

*Yado, of course, is only appreciated by a very private and tiny group of students and their teachers.*

The rest of the family went for a long weekend in Tokyo while I was to stay with Hiroshu sensei. I was looking forward to seeing him again as well as practicing yado with other students, students I had known for years, so I started out early in the morning for Nara.

I was surprised when sensei didn't greet me himself, but not so surprised to be met by Yoshimoro sensei, the teacher I had met in Kentucky at the medical center. I was asked to start practicing with the others and told I would meet with sensei later. I left my present for sensei and walked with

Hiroshu sensei to the nondescript building that was our secret dojo.

I was given a hood similar to those worn by bunraku puppet masters, a device that let me see out without exposing my features. This was something we had used many times in the past, a way of making us concentrate on anticipating our opponent's moves without relying on facial clues or eye movements. When he and I entered the practice hall I noted that all the other students were also hooded—again, not unusual. I suspected the hoods had something to do with masking my sight, but I didn't think it would hamper me. We were all used to anticipating an opponent's attack in many different ways.

After warming up he put us through a series of exercises, then left us to study on our own. I was amazed at the enhanced capabilities of these people and felt more than a little jealous they had been able to study almost daily with each other for all these years. I had developed a few tricks of my own in my solitary practice, though, and we quickly engrossed ourselves in the business of learning, flowing together in contention. I could tell the identities of some of the other students because of their signature movements, their habitual patterns, but was careful not to identify them by name. I felt so relaxed and at home here—the time passed much too quickly.

It was heaven to work with and oppose people who knew their art well. The flow of practice carried us well into the afternoon before there was a break called by Yoshimoro sensei. He talked with me for a few moments as the others left, then asked if I would mind practicing with him alone. We started, without hoods, after a short tea break for me, and I was kept busy again.

After about two hours I started to tire. I asked sensei for a break, but instead was asked to sit with him for instruction. He and I sat formally in kiza, sitting on our knees and toes, and he instructed me for a long time in the ways that banished weariness, that drew energy up from the inner core. Well after dark he continued to teach me complex exercises, ways to grow beyond my capabilities, ways to expand my self by losing myself.

*I felt the lessons take hold—they suddenly made sense, opening new doors for me. It was as if I had been studying the alphabet all these years and was suddenly able to read—not only words, but sentences, paragraphs, whole tomes—not just grasping the individual words but comprehending the meaning of everything I read.*

*Techniques and lessons that would have consumed months, if not years, were passed to me as quickly as water is poured from a pitcher to a glass, and new subtle shifts in movement and energy with my opponent became almost immediately apparent.*

Yoshimoro sensei finally called a break. We ate a simple meal of rice and vegetables, then relieved ourselves, washed, and took an ofuro, soaking in the too-hot water, relaxing. After the bath I was told to sleep for the few hours remaining until just before first light.

We began our practice again at dawn after a light meal, whirling and striking, defending and attacking, moving faster and more deliberately as the hours wore on. I seemed somehow to learn even better than before, absorbing new training easily and hungrily, understanding things almost instantly. The energy I felt seemed to flow through me like I was a garden hose, a conduit carrying something vital.

After an afternoon break I was again allowed to bathe, then presented with a formal black kimono and pin-striped gray hakama, common for men in ceremonial situations—the kimono decorated with five simple but elegant mon, although I wasn't familiar with the crest.

We walked the short distance to Hiroshu sensei's home, and I was blinded by late-afternoon light as we exited the dojo—I had practiced strenuous yado for most of thirty-six hours with only short breaks, and I felt wonderful!

Yoshimoro sensei left me at sensei's door as we bowed low to each other in very deep respect. I had gained a great deal of admiration for him in a short period of time and hoped we would meet again soon.

Hiroshu sensei seemed genuinely glad to see me, looking deeply into my eyes for a long time. He seemed to be satisfied with what he saw there. We settled on the veranda, both familiar with the pattern of our rituals, even though we had not shared them for over two years.

He carried the gift I had left on my arrival, a set of yado shafts I had made. They were burnished Cedar footed with Cocobolo and nocked with Tagua nut, a dense vegetable-based ivory that was much more durable than the real thing. I had developed a technique to airbrush realistic and permanent color into white feathers, and the fletching on these shafts looked more like eagle feathers than the now-unobtainable real ones would have. I had the display box made to match the shafts, even lining it with a matching velvet, and the effect was stunning at the same time it was simple—no wasted colors or parts, no extra ornamentation.

I had been very careful to match all the parts and pieces to one another, to use all the experience I had gained from making arrows over the years to make something I hoped he would appreciate.

He was amazed, bowing to me in appreciation after he studied their details. I gratefully returned his bow, then explained how they were crafted, even including the process used for the feathers. I assured him I took great spiritual care to create a special set of feathers, even if they weren't real.

"When you paint the picture of a flower, Maaku sensei, do you expect the viewer to think it is really a flower?"

I was shaken. "Hiroshu sensei, did you call me 'sensei?'"

"Yes, of course. There is still much to learn, but there is also time. We'll discuss many things today—please don't be impatient, and please answer my question."

Whew. "Sensei, when I paint a flower it is not to fool the viewer, but to call attention to the flower as I see it—to point out what I see as special. Perhaps it is the impression of movement in the wind, or what the flower feels like when it is covered with dew, or perhaps another aspect of the flower others might not see—maybe even a relationship between the flower and its surroundings."

Sensei studied the fletching. "When I look at these feathers I see something created just for these shafts.

"I see subtle color differences that tell me the arrows are the end result—not the feathers—and that the fletch are an important part of the whole. As an artist you could not help but to create these not just to mimic the feather of a powerful eagle, but to create a work of art meant to be more than the sum of its parts. I shall always treasure these—thank you." He bowed again, as did I.

"It is important for you to understand that intentions are what carry importance, much more so than deeds. These arrows are but one indication that you have become adept at merging the two.

"If you had not left daily training to return to your country, things would have been very different. As it was, you left here only partially trained, but a good enough student to continue learning on your own—that much is evident. Your situation is unique. Your were, in a sense, a child that was allowed to play with a poisonous snake, and, in spite of that you have made many right decisions.

"What is important now is to make sure you have the proper training, something we will discuss a great deal while you are here."

I knew he had my best interest at heart, so I centered myself for a few moments, then started from the beginning, relating all my self-learned lessons, doubts, and fears over the past two years. It was a long day.

*Hiroshu sensei explained that it was important for me to have public status as a sensei and that officially I would test to be a teacher of kyudo. The scheduled exam would be held in less than a week, a very busy week full of practice and meditation.*

*Henmi sensei was still my archery teacher, and had trained me through the years up through fifth dan, the rank that was a prerequisite for taking the teaching exam. He was aware of my yado training, but had made it clear that this week was about kyudo, nothing else. My new position, if I passed, would be a critical part of my continuing growth, an open gate to new and larger lessons.*

*"To teach something is to confirm our own learning—that is why it is important to teach what you know to someone else," Henmi sensei told me during one of our many training sessions. "You have spent many years learning each small lesson and overcoming your own fears. You will now find out what it is like to help others with the same lessons. I understand that you have been training your wife, which is a good start, yet not the objective teaching you must now study.*

*"You know that a sensei's responsibility is more to a student's inner self than to the outer, but you may not know what this means on a day-to-day basis.*

*"It does not matter in the long run whether someone studies kyudo or not. The lessons an individual needs to learn may best be studied in another forum entirely—that's why it's important to evaluate someone carefully before accepting them as a student. Each individual has motives for wanting to learn, and you must judge the merit of those motives, to judge whether kyudo is the proper art for that person. This ability to judge will come with practice and time, with meditation and a properly reflective spirit.*

*"The more closely connected we are to our center, the subtler the things that engage us—the more disconnected we are, the louder something has to be to attract our attention.*

*"Most people assume a person is like a body of water—either shallow and wide or narrow and deep. This is indeed true for most people: Some*

*immerse themselves deeply in an art or a discipline to the exclusion of everything else, diving as far towards their own center as they may, while others never commit deeply to anything, never even realize there is a deeper life. You will come to see this is true.*

*"It is also true at each stage of development. If a student is at first eager to learn it is a wonderful experience, but it may also be a wonderful trap, keeping the student happily engaged, not seeing the need for further growth, further depth. The distractions of our lives are always enough to keep us busy. At any fully-realized stage it is always more difficult to explore further.*

*"It will be your job to assess these levels in your students and in yourself, to enjoy your attainments while diving ever deeper, to keep yourself centered while remaining open to new expansion.*

*"Foremost, understand that safety always comes first."*

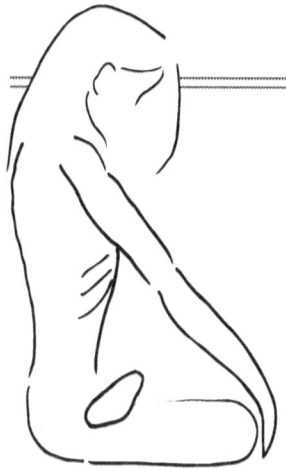

## The Eve of the Millennia

# Florida

*Patience. Strength without tension.*

*In the Western world, many archers feel that their own style of practice is the only form of real archery. The self bow shooters feel that those that use composite longbows are cheating; American longbow archers feel that reproduction recurve shooters are using an unfair mechanical advantage; historic recurve shooters aren't fond of those who use a shelf on their bow to rest the arrow; modern traditional recurve shooters call the cabled cams at the ends of a compound bow "training wheels;" and compound shooters who use mechanical releases think that crossbows are only for the lazy.*

*We all shoot at the same target, all feel the same sense of satisfaction when an arrow flies well.*

Another just-after-Christmas winter, sitting on the same porch of the same house on the same lake, watching my children play with each other in the same way they always had, though they threw Frisbees this late December instead of swimming in the chilly water.

There were differences now, of course, and it was difficult to forget a time when there were four children next to the lake instead of just three—we would always hurt for our Samantha, always remember her as the little nine year old Tinkerbell that she had been, never allowed to grow into an adult.

The other children had grown, though.

Jessica, almost eighteen, had developed into an amazingly beautiful woman, inside and out. Hanna, a precocious fifteen, was beautiful too, beautiful and feisty—ready to begin taking on the world of young men, she thought. Young Mark was just breaking into the teenage years, ready not to be the baby anymore—a bit gawky still, it was easy to see glimpses of the capable, handsome, and caring man he was to become. I was proud of my children—they were good people.

A very pregnant Melissa and I had been here two months preparing for tonight, while the children had stayed with their grandmother in Kentucky attending their own schools, visiting us on weekends. This was to be our fifth child and fourth home birth, so things were old hat now—but still a little scary for both of us.

We wanted to have this bunkin here at the lake, but hadn't had the heart to transfer the kids to new schools for just a few months. They had flown down to be with us as soon as Christmas vacation started, and we would all go home in the RV as soon as we were done and rested. This was still only really a family vacation place for us, but remained a very important part of our lives, especially mine.

I had planned this series of events for a long time, and tonight should be the night, with assistance from many sources. Everything was theoretically ready for the birth, but experience told me that things were never really ready enough for an expectant mother—there was always something that could stand tweaking.

I knew I would have to go into the house shortly to deal with a bustling Melissa, but she knew I had something important to do first, and knew she could reach me easily if she needed.

I studied the new dojo set close to the side of the house as I walked over, admiring the traditional Japanese construction, simple but roughly elegant and almost two years in the making.

Usually a dojo would consist of two buildings with openings that faced each other across twenty-eight meters, one for the shooting platform, viewing stand, practice target, and equipment storage, the other much smaller structure for the targets themselves. I had the design altered so it was now a single long structure, though, to make a display space for a site-based sculpture that was installed in the ceiling space between the shooter and the target.

Entering the dojo and leaving off the lights, I sat on the shooting platform for ten or fifteen minutes to study the sculpture, to meditate. It was going to be a busy night, and I wanted to be calm and well-centered.

The artist had accurately reproduced the five boat frames from Oak and Poplar using plans of old Viking vessels, a tribute to my own blond heritage. The keels of the boat frames had been copper-clad, then the inside of each had been covered with natural-hued canvas to form a translucent inner "skin." When raised to various heights close to the high ceiling and lit with small translucent skylights directly above each, the sculpture looked for all the world like graceful and magical spirit ships carrying souls on their trip to the other world, ships that lit the dojo with an incredible unearthly glow, relaxing and inspiring. The complex yet graceful backlit skeletons of the boats were more than visible, the copper keels reflecting the light in subtle counterpoints. Black cloth surrounded each skylight, running down in an upside-down funnel shape that was then connected all around the inside of the top edge of each boat. As the sunlight outside changed the concentrated lights inside each craft would change as well, allowing the muted patterns waving back and forth on the floor to mimic waves of light that shone down through water, as well as lighting the mist target at the far end with a soft glow. There were rheostatically-controlled lights inside each boat for night use, and a spotlight for highlighting the target, if I wished.

The original installation had required eleven tons of rock salt to cover the floor, but I had changed that to white beach sand so any arrows that didn't reach the target wouldn't be harmed. From the edge of the raised shooting platform all the way to the far end of the building, the sand was piled in apparently casual heaps that resembled the undulating lake bottom I loved so well—small hills and valleys spotted with pools of warm light from the vessels above.

When I was a little younger than Mark is now I would sit on the bottom of the close-by lake as long as I could, trying to look up at the boats passing overhead, loving the way they cut through the water. Granted, I couldn't stay down very long, but I gave it my best shot, taking a big breath and diving down to sit cross-legged just before they would pass over. I was never sure what the fascination was for me, but I never got tired of sitting down there.

Now I had a place of my own to re-dream those days, always able to watch the boats passing overhead, now even better without the danger of being hit by a ski boat. This was my personal center, a place to always be my inner home.

I wondered what Mom would have said those many years ago if she had caught me on the bottom of the lake, speeding boats passing above me.

*I watched the flame on the floor before me, let the ingredients of my internal stew react with each other.*

*Images tumbled over and through themselves, concepts formed and disappeared.*

*Studying the candle, I felt at times like I was watching a star in the night sky, an unobtainable target too far to ever know. At other moments the light felt close enough to burn me, something I could reach out and touch. It changed from one view to another from time to time, and I knew it was trying to communicate with me, to tell me what I already knew.*

*I took careful breaths, drew the air deep down into my diaphragm and then let it slowly out, centering myself even more. I wanted to absorb what was happening, to feel it within my whole being.*

*I imagined the heat from the flame being drawn in as I inhaled, then out again to heat the already warm space around me.*

*I enlarged the breath area to include the target twenty-eight meters distant, rested, then imagined a bubble that enclosed the dojo with warmth and light.*

*I reached out then to Melissa and the bunkins, feeling them, wishing them light, enlarging the bubble even more. The bubble now fully included my core, my essence—I rested in it, readied myself.*

*I remembered other individuals important to me, most too far away for a breath or a bubble. I felt each individual, asleep or awake, near or far, felt them accept my small benediction.*

*I was in the center of a network of special people and I connected to each one. I extended my self—thought by thought, space by space—extended that central part of myself until I surrounded the globe, touched many places.*

*The network merged to became a globe itself, a sphere of personal energy that held a connection for each being. Suddenly I felt the world the way it should be, a Garden of Eden, the special place that was promised.*

*Thy Kingdom Come. Thy will be done in earth, as it is in Heaven.*

*I sat for a time with my eyes half-closed, feeling this idealized world while making a star out of the small candle, feeling the variety of the earth with each breath through to my center.*

*I watched the flame riding on top of the ever-smaller taper.*

*Every decision is a creative decision, everything we make from our personal center is art for us.*

There was only one more thing to check. My yumi and other kyudo equipment were in the dojo, patiently waiting in a display rack. The bow had been strung and used enough so that I was sure of its performance, and the fire arrows stood in their rack, ready to be set aflame.

Covered in traditional cattails at the tip, they would burn rapidly when doused in kerosene and lit. As they burned they would quickly consume the underlying sheath that covered the white phosphorus core, a core that would then burn with a light bright enough to be seen far away.

I had spent a great deal of time on these shafts, wanting them to reflect the importance of their use, to me if no one else. Each one had been patiently crafted and tuned to my yumi, and I expected to retrieve each shaft from the lake after it had been used. I hoped to give the first one to the new child to keep for posterity.

It was time to embrace Melissa.

*Except for Mark, my youngest, each of my children had seen and participated in our home birth process, had each helped deliver a baby. While this pregnancy was a surprise it was welcome nonetheless, a merging together of all the natural events of our amazing lives.*

*Jessica had come through Melissa in a birthing center with no complications, and after that we were only comfortable at home, building our own traditions with each new child. We almost had to have home births—I became so protective when one of my children was being birthed that I couldn't stand to have someone else in the room, no matter how knowledgeable or professional. We had tried midwives, but even they were too intrusive. Missy understood and was even proud of my concern—sometimes.*

*The price I paid for wanting a home birth was medical research, refreshing my knowledge with each new child. It was important that my darling have faith in me, and anything I could do to help her with that faith was worth it.*

The rest of the day was spent checking final preparations. We had removed the bed from the ground floor bedroom and replaced it with a new futon on top of a mattress. The top of the futon was surrounded with pillows of every size, firmness, and shape for Melissa's comfort, and there was a stack of sheets and quilts next to it in plastic bags, to keep them clean. We used the bureau in the corner to hold some extra comfort items, small things that we wanted to keep close but didn't want to sterilize. Next to the bureau there was a rolling table covered with both the necessary medical supplies and the knife to be used to cut the umbilicus. Everything on this table was sterilized and sealed, then checked against a master list.

I looked at the knife and chuckled. It was a handmade tanto, a personal-sized knife traditionally carried by the Japanese—a present from Hiroshu sensei just for this child, the handle and sheath made from burled rosewood, quite unusual for a Japanese knife. It was a beautiful gift and it would perform well tonight, but it looked so out of place next to all the modern medical supplies that it tickled me.

The knife itself had been sterilized and vacuum-sealed in a clear plastic envelope, and that bothered me some—I worried that it couldn't breathe, oddly enough. Just a little longer now, little knife—if your sterilization reassured Melissa, then you'd just have to hold your breath for awhile.

This was one of the traditions that we had created in our lives together. Each child's cord had been cut with their own knife, then engraved with the event, child's name, and date. Our intention was to hand each knife down to its true owner when they left home, presumably after college or—even better—at marriage. For now the other knives were locked in a special display case at home. The children took pride in their knives, handling them and polishing them periodically. No matter what else our family had, our children were most proud of what these knives represented—it was a good tradition.

We had discussed reusing Samantha's knife for this child, but decided against it. Birthing this child here was part of the healing process after losing Sam, as was having another child at all, but we didn't want to emphasize that to this new person that we would see for the first time tonight. Sam's knife would be a permanent reminder for the rest of our lives, a small altar.

Melissa was in the kitchen now, making sure the kids and I would have enough to eat in the next several hours, even though we were all perfectly capable of feeding ourselves. She just needed to feel ready, so we let her arrange and fuss and rearrange and re-fuss until she was happy.

The bed area looked for all the world like a nest because of all the pillows. I had noticed this nesting instinct before, both with Missy and others. An expectant mother needed to give birth in a place that she felt was safe and nurturing, as far from danger as could be managed. She needed to be relaxed and ready for the birth to happen with her full cooperation. This bed was her center, at least for now—this is where she would bring this new life to our family.

There shouldn't be any more risk with this delivery than any of the others. True, my bride was now in her early forties, but there was no way for anyone to determine that except by asking—she was still youthful-looking and well-toned, in fantastic shape.

At eight o'clock we started our birth ceremony, as much a part of our tradition as anything else.

We started by showering together, each making sure that the other was very clean. We took our time with the shower, enjoying it, calming ourselves while becoming excited. We had all the time in the world. I was counting on the timing of her performance based on her other deliveries—she had always taken the same amount of time with each delivery after her first.

After we finished washing I reached outside the shower stall and got the new flip-flops, broke the package seal, then put them on the floor so I could step into them. Outside the stall I unsealed two large fluffy towels, drying myself and then my Missy, after she had put on her own pair of new flip-flops. After we brushed our teeth and I shaved we moved to the bedroom and shut the door, happy and clean.

This part of the birth was ours alone. We would call in the children when it was time.

We stayed naked for now, my clothes ready on top of the pile of quilts along with her nightshirt. We both abandoned the flip-flops and got into bed sitting with crossed legs, facing each other—she couldn't cross hers in exactly the same way as she could when her belly was flat, but had found a comfortable position that she could hold for a while.

We meditated then with our eyes open, each of us staring deeply into the other. I matched my rate of breath to hers as I had so many times before, holding her hands gently, making myself a part of her.

Rising back to the surface, I looked consciously into her eyes, caring for her, accepting her, valuing her, watching her love return to me, feeling her acceptance of the healing power we shared.

After a time I caressed her hands slowly, bringing her back, starting our ceremony. This was our time to say very private things to each other, things that no one else would ever hear, and we made good use of it.

We talked like this for a time, saying our special things, then my caresses began exploring her body, relaxing her, exciting her.

I had her lie down on her back, propped with pillows, then massaged her from head to toe, exploring her completely. It was important for her to fully realize how deeply I felt about her, how much I accepted her, how much she could count on me. I spent a lot of time on her aching legs and feet to calm them down, appreciating them fully, then, moving my left hand gently up her leg and inside her thigh, I started massaging her, slowly at first.

Even though she expected my touch, she jumped slightly. Sex to initiate birth was important for us, the official start of the physical process, and perhaps a little scary for that. It showed her emotional self that I loved her, it told her physical self that I was there and involved—all of her births had begun with sex, even Jessica's. Our first birth process, it had surprised us that she started her contractions when she had an orgasm. Once we knew it, though, we took full advantage, using sex to begin the process each time. We had developed our birth ceremony as a signal to her deeper self that we were ready to receive this child, a ceremony more cunningly crafted than even our marriage had been.

She had to be physically ready, of course, and she was, the bunkin inside fully formed and ready to appear.

Birthing was something that we truly did together. The birth itself was something that only she could do, but it wouldn't have been the same process without my love. The same was true of anything that I created, as well—I was the one that birthed the works of art, but it wouldn't have been the same process if she hadn't supported me, believed in me, loved me. I had missed her so much when she was away from me in a coma, and I held to her even tighter now because of that.

Once she settled to my touch, I kissed her deeply, sharing breath with her, loving her. I felt her acceptance of my touch and my love, felt her relax to my control—I knew that it was important to her that I be gentle and sensitive, but it was also critical that she knew I was in control now, both of her body and of the situation.

My touch became completely sexual now, letting her know how badly I desired her, continuing for several minutes.

It didn't take long for her to come to orgasm like this, a deep shuddering wave that contracted her again and again as her water broke. Her womb tightened for the first time then as I kissed her neck, rubbed her, felt the warmth.

I helped her up to wash again, then cleaned up the area, changing the sheets and protective pad. Before she got back into the bed I unsealed her new flannel floor-length nightshirt and helped her into it. It was roomy and open enough at the bottom to allow full access to me during the birth, loose enough at the top to feed the baby after the birth.

I laid her back down, covered her with sheets and a warm quilt, made sure she was comfortable. I got dressed in my clean clothes, then kissed this person, my wife, kissed her with my full attention. This was probably our last time alone for awhile.

Only then did I open the door to invite in the older kids.

Everyone was excited, but ready to handle their jobs well. Jessica was Assistant Number One—her assignment was to help me to deal with Missy's bottom half. Hanna's and Mark's jobs as Assistant Number Two and Three was support their mother's upper needs—keeping her supplied with water and ice chips, washing her face with a damp cloth, having hands squeezed permanently out of shape. No hospital ever provided a more supportive crew.

As the contractions became more severe, we all helped Missy to focus, to calm, to breathe. She had been trained to accept the pain, to let it wash through her, but the training only worked to a certain point—the point where the pain became a solid core, making her as completely filled with it as anyone could ever be. I had an unbelievable respect for her, for anyone brave enough to give birth, to go through this pain.

When she was dilated far enough I allowed her to push, then watched her carefully as the head slowly appeared, just as it should. The progress was agonizingly slow until the widest part of the head passed, then I was rushing to check the position of the cord and support a new little face-down body at the same time, moving in as calculated a manner as I ever had in performing a martial arts kata.

I turned the baby over, holding the head in my hands, supporting the body with my forearms, checking him for any visible impairments as I rubbed him to awaken his cries.

As I looked into his face I remembered a line from the television series *Designing Women*. A pregnant Charlene was taking a nap, not knowing that it was about time for her to start to deliver her baby, when she had a dream of her Guardian Angel—Dolly Parton, of all people—who told her something that had stuck with me ever since: "Remember—this new little person that you're meeting for the first time is the one who'll be holding your hand when it's your turn to go."

Whatever else happened in my life, the birth of each of my children showed me the real wonder of the universe, gave me the most pure joy.

Blood-covered and seeing through a thick layer of tears, I announced to my family and the world that we had another son. They gathered around in excited silence to see his face as I kneeled there, transfixed for a few moments.

Hanna looked over at the clock and almost screamed as she realized what she saw. "We made it, everybody! We made it! He was born twelve seconds after midnight!

"Happy New Millennium, everybody!"

I hushed her as we all got busy making sure both Mother and Child were well, as Missy hungrily absorbed the sight of her new son.

When things calmed down, the afterbirth delivered, the cord cut, the knife cleaned, the placenta placed in a plastic bag and sent out with the kids, Melissa and I snuggled together on the bed and looked into his blue eyes as she held him in his little blanket—it was time to find out who he was.

We never named a child until we could see his-or-her face.

"So," she said, "who do we have here?"

I looked at his little serious face and studied him. "He looks like a 'Matthew' to me. What do you think?"

She studied him. "Matthew—I like it. Done." She looked at his face again, stroked it with a mother's finger. "He's had a big day."

"Well," she said, exhaling, still looking at his face, his little eyes now closed. "We made it into the new year for the birth."

"Yup."

"Think we were the first?"

"I don't know."

I looked into her eyes, then bent down and kissed her, a quiet moment for both of us. "Happy New Year, new Mother."

"Happy New Year to you, new Daddy." Her face turned serious.

"Are you going to go out for the middle name now?"

"In a minute—I've got a little surprise first."

"Oh, goody. For me?"

"Sort of." I brought a small peat cup over from the bureau, a little sprout growing up a few inches above the surface of the dirt. I tilted the cup gently so she could see the plant.

"You're right. That is about the littlest surprise I've ever seen."

"Not so big now, it's true," I admitted. "But it will be. This is grown from an acorn from the Treaty Oak in Jacksonville, and I thought we could plant it over the placenta. Okay?"

"Oh, Darling, I'd forgotten about the planting—how sweet! Are we going to plant it here?

"Yup! We can pick a place with plenty of room tomorrow."

"Plenty of room?"

"Sure. We don't want to come back every few hundred years to prune the damn thing, now do we? If it grows as big as its daddy it'll be over two hundred feet across."

*I checked in with the kids, shared the baby's first name, joined in the excitement, celebrated, got Jessica and Hanna started on the phone spreading the news. After about an hour, when things had quieted down a bit and the doctor had left, I got a cup of coffee and picked a favorite Canadian-style pipe from the rack, then went outside alone. Another part of our tradition, this one borrowed from the Native Americans.*

*It was now my job to see what was special about this time and place, to determine my new child's power, to pick his middle name. An unhurried process, I usually gained a great deal of insight.*

*This was my time to be alone with myself, to look inward as well as outward, a time respected by my family. I sat on the porch swing to drink coffee and to smoke, enjoying the mild night, occasional flashes of fireworks visible from time to time. This was probably the biggest party night of anyone alive now, a celebration of the start of a new thousand years.*

*When I was finished with the coffee I filled my bowl again, lit the pipe, and walked down the gradual sandy grass slope to the edge of the lake, watching and listening to the night, disturbing the crickets into silence. I stood there awhile, next to a lonely, gnarled, and smoothly weathered tree that tried to prosper too close to the water, its sparse and leafless branches curling upward above me.*

*I heard a snake as he slid his winding path through the patch of weeds next to the tree, watched a cloud of my smoke slowly drift out over the water. I saw and heard the night insects and birds going about their business, felt the consistency of the sand under my bare feet. I smelled wood smoke from someone's fireplace—a neighbor, perhaps, trying to convince his family that it was cold enough for a nice fire.*

*I sat down to meditate, keeping my eyes open. The longer I sat, the more sounds came to my ears.*

*To be accepted in a place it is necessary to become a part of that place—a universal law, one I sometimes fought. This small part of the universe didn't belong to me, belonged instead to the things and creatures who existed here—I was just a visitor. No matter how much I thought of the lake as my early home, my interests took me too far afield for me to be only here, to feel only here.*

*A field mouse broke into a tiny run away from me, dodging back and forth, an odd thing to happen at night. The sound of his run through the grass halted abruptly.*

*The air smelled like air should, the sand felt like sand was meant to feel, the water wet me like water was supposed to—different, somehow, than other air, other sand, other waters. I relaxed into that feeling, then extended my self, first down into the earth, then to the space around me, then up and out. I became this place, absorbed the thousands of activities and details around me, felt the still things breathe.*

*Matthew was of this place, even more than I was. I brought him and his connections in to me, integrated this child to his first home, waited for the knowledge of who he was.*

*I heard a noise in the tree, slowly turned my head up to see a Red-tailed Hawk resting there, staring at me with a fixed stare.*

*Still staring, he stretched himself up and out to show his full wingspan as if to call my attention, then relaxed. He left the branch, taking off, flying away from me into the night.*

I joined my family in the bedroom, where everyone was watching my son eat. We were all tired, Missy especially, but we were also excited.

I picked him up then announced, "I would like to introduce you all to Matthew NightHunter, the newest member of our family."

Cheers and stories followed. To see a hawk was rare enough, but it must certainly be a special sign to see one at night, especially up close.

We all soon started to feel the fatigue. I helped Missy to the quilt-covered porch swing where she could see the lake, then helped Hanna give the baby to his mother. When they were comfortable, I went to the dojo, still barefoot, and went through the ritual of donning my shooting glove, lacing it carefully while kneeling. When this was properly done, I picked up the bow and a fire arrow, then went back outside, stopping just past the door to dip the cattail in a jar of kerosene.

*I walked down to the edge of the lake a little way past our usual spot, past the lone and naked tree I had just visited, down to a point where the shoreline formed the inner part of a boomerang shape, the lake itself bending back to either side. It was four hundred yards to the far edge.*

*I kneeled for a few moments to ready myself, then stood and prepared to shoot in the proper manner. When I was ready, Mark used my lighter to ignite the tip, then retreated a few yards to stand next to Hanna. Melissa, Jessica, and Matthew watched from the porch.*

*I raised the bow and deliberately drew, push-pulling until the bow was at full draw, the glove back by my shoulder, the tension within me as bright as the tip's flame and as dark as the night. I elevated the arrow's tip to a steep angle for maximum flight distance and held for a few moments, releasing just as the now-uncovered white phosphorus started to burn. I watched the bright whiteness trail in a wondrous arc through the sky, pushed by my special shaft. I thought I briefly saw a flying shadow near the arrow as it flew.*

*I held my final extended position until well after the arrow silently fell back down and slipped beneath the surface, dove far out into the lake—much more than far enough.*

*"So long as the new moon returns in heaven a bent, beautiful bow, so long will the fascination of archery keep hold of the hearts of men."*

—Maurice Thompson,
*The Witchery of Archery*, 1879